CAPTAINS

Captains

Sanford H. Margalith

JoNa Books
Bedford, IN

ISBN 09657929-8-6
Library of Congress Number 00 131105

First Printing June 2001

For Betty

Some of this happened.

Some of this should have happened.

Some of this should not have happened.

Chapter 1

Cora Lee Cadgett, bony and blonde, stared down at her daughter and frowned.

"Suck up them corn flakes," she ordered, "That Japanese fella will be here any second. Don't want to be late for church, hear?"

"Gosh, Mamma, I'm eating as fast as I can," Mara Cadgett answered. Tow-headed like her mother and contrary like her father, she was scrawny by nature and pale to near albinism.

Outside their tiny apartment came the sound of an ailing Ford sedan, then a groan of neglected brakes as Kunioshi's taxi came to a stop.

Cora Lee opened the door before Kunioshi had a chance to knock.

"And how are you this fine Sunday morning, Mrs. Cadgett?" he asked, pulling his Hawaiian shirt from his damp torso with one hand while smoothing the wrinkles from his chino trousers with the other. Though Kunioshi appeared Japanese and nothing but Japanese, he had enough European blood in him to startle people with his indigo eyes.

"Fair to middlin'," Cora Lee replied, and pushing her dawdling daughter before her, got into the back seat of the cab.

"I'd offer you a cup of coffee if there was time," Cora Lee remarked after settling back in the lumpy seat. She said that every Sunday, but she knew she could never bring herself to do it.

"Mr. Cadgett have the duty today?" Kunioshi

7

asked.

Cora Lee was annoyed. Kunioshi knew full well that that was the only reason her husband would be absent from his family on a Sunday.

Instead of answering, Cora Lee turned her attention to the sound of explosions and the banging of guns coming from the distant east.

"Gunnery practice," she commented.

"Anchors aweigh!" Kunioshi said, and drove down the road leading out of the working class neighborhood, one place in Honolulu a Navy enlisted man's family could afford if the husband was willing to commute the thirty miles to his ship by bus.

On both sides of the road, tropical growth flourished. Flowers emerging from the tangled greenery were the targets of swooping butterflies. Rotting vegetation and the strong scent of flowers filled the air with a cloying odor.

Kunioshi's sun-faded brown cab displayed a Hawaiian hula girl on both front doors. Above their heads was the legend KUNIOSHI TAXI CO. HONOLULU, and below their bare feet the telephone number in bright orange.

"You look mighty spiffy today, Mara," Kunioshi said, paying no attention to Cora Lee's observation about the gunfire.

The condescension in Kunioshi's tone irritated Cora Lee. She frowned as she watched her daughter look down proudly at her new plaid skirt and starched white blouse.

"My daddy bought it for me," the girl said. "It's my new Sunday-go-to-meetin' outfit. He had it on layaway till now. Don't you go to church, Mr. Kunioshi?"

"Religion's okay," was his answer.

"You can come to our church."

"The Jehovah's Witnesses or the Seventh Day Adventists, maybe," he said.

"Reverend Parker says you must accept Christ as your savior, Mr. Kunioshi. "To be saved, I mean. Isn't that right, Mamma?"

Cora Lee did not hear her daughter's question.

8

She was totally absorbed in the racket from the harbor.

"I'll consider that, young lady, yes, I will," said Kunioshi.

Kunioshi began to slow the taxi as soon as the First Southern Baptist Church of Hawaii came into sight.

The roar of aircraft grew so loud Cora Lee covered her ears with her hands. Her knees were pressed together. Her prim white collar gaped from her bosom revealing a spangle of orange freckles above her blue church dress.

"I wish them fliers would show a little consideration for us folks on the ground," she said.

And then Cora Lee was dead; Mara and Kunioshi, too.

Chapter II

Only moments before, Quartermaster First Class Verne Cadgett stepped onto the bridge of the USS *Bear Mountain* to relieve Quartermaster Third Class Jim McNabb.

"You're late, Verne," McNabb said.

This was as critical as McNabb dared get with Cadgett. Even officers held back from hazing the man, a sinuous Kentuckian whose grim gray eyes ranged penetratingly over men, stripping them of much of their bravado and pretense. Cadgett had risen fast in the Navy. It was as if his superiors were appeasing him with promotions, much as one would pacify a dangerous animal with offerings of red meat.

"Secure, will you?" Cadgett said, "Technically I ain't late yet." He held up his hawser of an arm so McNabb could see his wrist watch.

The watch was new and much too expensive for Cadgett, but he had been so captivated by the blue anchor on its dial that he could not resist buying it. It showed a few minutes to eight, with the second handle jerking toward the numeral twelve.

A sudden blast of scorching hot air dissolved the watch's crystal before their eyes. The almost simultaneous explosion that followed smashed McNabb and the Officer of the Deck, Lieutenant Walter Zimmer, against the bulkhead and hurled Cadgett out of the bridge's blown-open hatch, over the ship's side, and into the harbor. The Aichi dive bomber that scored the hit just behind the *Bear Mountain*'s smokestack went on to strafe road traffic in Honolulu, then flew off to the north.

Cadgett's head bobbed up out of water already

darkening with oil from his crippled ship. The explosion had forced blood from his nose and burnt his back. Despite those minor wounds and a badly bruised leg and shoulder, he could still maneuver in the water. Cadgett wiped the blood and muck from his eyes and took in the scene around him. He was astonished that he had been propelled so far from his burning ship by the explosion and had survived. Smoke shot upward from stricken ships and hung like greasy, black thunderclouds above the wounded vessels. The water was cluttered with flotsam: life jackets, bits of uniforms, pieces of wood, and hunks of human flesh. In the midst of all that, Cadgett watched men struggle and drown, while those who could, swam to the safety of hastily launched boats. Sailors and Marines, scalded by burning fuel oil or escaping steam, screamed for help. Cadgett's lungs convulsed from the acrid chemistry of exploding bombs, his eyes stung from vapors given off by heat-peeled paint, and there was the odor of burnt flesh in his nostrils.

Choosing the largest piece of floating debris, the top of a mess table, Cadgett swam to it and grabbed on. Flailing arms churned the water nearby and Cadgett recognized Bert Sutherland, one of the *Bear Mountain*'s boatswain's mates who had shared the watch with him and McNabb.

"Over here!" Cadgett shouted to Sutherland.

When Sutherland reached the tabletop raft, he seized hold with both hands.

"Ammunition ship blow up?" Sutherland asked, after he caught his breath.

Cadgett let one arm go from the tabletop and pointed up at a darkening sky.

Sutherland tilted his head back and followed Cadgett's hand with his eyes.

"Planes," Sutherland said, sounding puzzled.

"Japs," Cadgett said.

"Son of a bitch," Sutherland muttered.

"Seen any of the crew?" Cadgett asked.

"They're out there in the water. Those who are alive."

11

"And Zimmer?"

"Dead, I think. Him and McNabb."

"What you mean *think*?"

"I saw them after the explosion. When I came down from the signal bridge, they were laying there."

"Sure they're dead?"

"Want me to have waited around until a doctor pronounced them?"

Cadgett shook his head, sighed with disgust and pushed himself away from the tabletop.

"Where you going?" Sutherland called after him.

"Where you think?"

"You're going to drown man. She's sinking fast."

"Shut up, Sutherland!" Cadgett shouted, and swam away.

By the time Cadgett reached the *Bear Mountain* the ship had settled enough in the water so he didn't have to climb over the gunwale to get on the deck. He swam to the superstructure where he managed to grab a rung of the ladder to the bridge. Cadgett climbed up, sea water pouring from him, his clothing stained with oil. By now his bruised body began to hurt and he winced every inch of the way to the bridge. Inside he found Zimmer badly hurt, but far from dead. McNabb, however, lay lifeless.

"Goddamn Sutherland anyway!" he cried aloud, and grasped Zimmer under the armpits. Cadgett dragged the officer to the ladder where he waited until the rising water reached the level of the bridge. Then Cadgett slipped Zimmer into the water and dove in after him. He grabbed the unconscious officer around the chest and swam with him toward the makeshift raft. By this time, a rescue motor launch had plucked Sutherland from the harbor. Cadgett could make out Sutherland waving him in toward the launch as if he were a partner in the rescue. After Zimmer was pulled aboard, the launch moved around the harbor picking up survivors. When there was no more room, the boat made its way toward Ford Island.

"Why did you risk your life for that guy?" Sutherland asked Cadgett.

"I was following orders."

"Whose orders?"

"Mine, you stupid son of a bitch."

Together, Cadgett and the rest of the survivors watched stunned as the *Bear Mountain* turned belly up like a great fish, dead.

Approaching Ford Island, Cadgett could see the situation was no better there. The entire world seemed to be on fire. A pall hovered over the harbor, turning morning into eerie twilight.

By the time the launch tied up at Pier Ten Ten, an icy feeling came over Cadgett and his anger turned into a grim resolve.

Cadgett's thoughts went then to his wife Cora Lee. When they had met, she had been a waitress in a San Francisco coffee shop. The moment she asked for his order he recognized her as near kin. Cora Lee's father had brought her to the West Coast from eastern Kentucky just after her mother died because he heard there was work in California. Cadgett and Cora Lee's bond was more than a marriage. They were connected by the customs and myths of Appalachia, and when their daughter Mara was born their bond was made complete and uncompromising.

Cadgett was anxious to get to a phone and assure Cora Lee that he was all right.

CHAPTER III

In December, 1943, almost two years to the day after he found himself swimming in the flaming waters of Pearl Harbor, Lieutenant Verne Cadgett, newly-appointed captain of the USS LST *1525*, stood at attention on the deck of the new tank landing ship in New Orleans. First in the two rows of ribbons on his chest was the Silver Star, a decoration that Zimmer made sure Cadgett got for rescuing him. The medal had eased Cadgett's way into a commission, which was followed by two more promotions during the first years of the war.

The crew was mustered in two ranks on the starboard side of the deck, a chief boatswain's mate at their head. The vessel's junior officers stood in single file on the port side. Behind a portable lectern, Rear Admiral Roger L. Purdon, in command of the naval district, faced the ship's company. Behind him stood Lieutenant (j.g.) Taliaferro J. Brown, executive officer and second in command of the LST. The admiral was an old sea dog called out of retirement when war broke out. He was a small man, so slightly built he looked as if his cap would tip onto his face from the weight of the heavy gold braid on its visor. His face was red as raw meat and his chest glared with poly-chromatic campaign ribbons going back to the First World War. Purdon seemed in a hurry to finish and finally concluded with scarce effort to hide his relief.

"...now with the authority vested in me by the President of the United States, I hereby place the United States Ship LST *1525* in commission. God bless and God speed to all who sail in her."

When the admiral began to organize his papers in preparation for leaving, Brown went to the next step in the ceremony. "Ship's Company, Lieutenant Verne C. Cadgett, captain of the LST *1525*."

Cadgett replaced Purdon behind the lectern. His face was a slagheap, all angles and shadows. His gray eyes squinted at the assembled crew. They were mostly seventeen- to nineteen-year-olds. Some had never even seen the sea. They were boys who had been weaned on Coca-Cola, had dined out on Baby Ruths and quit high school to go to work in gas stations and grocery stores. The war saved them from marriage to the first girl artful enough to let them do it without a condom. Their baggy government issue dress blue uniforms made them look even more callow than they were, almost like children on a seaside holiday. To Cadgett, the officers were little better. They appeared to be a clutch of eager middle-class college boys.

There were a few aboard Cadgett could depend on. There was his chief boatswain's mate, with eight years destroyer duty behind him. Balding and thin as a ship's mast, Chief knew his job and brooked no nonsense. There was the engineering officer, Lieu-tenant (j.g.) Chester Craft, with hair so dark red it could pass for the color mahogany. He had solid ex-perience on a variety of diesel-engined auxiliary ves-sels and was one of the two officers aboard, besides Cadgett, above the rank of ensign. The other was Lieutenant Brown, Cadgett's executive officer. He had been a Richmond, Virginia insurance salesman, a descendent of Judd J. Rhodes, a storied Confederate cavalry officer. But no one could mistake Brown for

15

a warrior. Nor was there anything of the mariner about him. Narrow shouldered, with a belly showing a feminine-like swell, he walked with a near shuffle and spoke in a plaintive squeak. His heavy beard always made Brown look a day behind in shaving. His eyes blinked continuously and he reminded Cadgett of nothing so much as a sweating embezzler.

The ship's company stared back at their captain, lips pale, eyes pleading for information. After a long silence, Cadgett spoke. "You wanted a glamour ship. A PT boat, a destroyer. Maybe you wanted a battleship because you heard they have a soda fountain on board and you could stuff your gut with gedunk. You got an LST. Know what they're called? Large Slow Targets."

Leaving them to ponder his words, Cadgett turned and delivered the required salute to Admiral Purdon. "I report for duty as commanding officer."

Purdon returned the scripted courtesy.

Now it was Brown's turn to shout an order, and he did so with high-pitched gusto. "Hoist the colors!"

Up the halyard went the American flag. And that was it. There was none of the peacetime pageantry, no band playing "Anchors Aweigh".

Disappointment darkened Brown's face. He turned and whispered to Cadgett, "That was one chicken shit commissioning."

Brown's whisper was overheard by Purdon, who hurried from the ship without stopping to shake Cadgett's hand and wish him luck.

***

To Admiral Purdon's annoyance he found he had to visit the LST *1525* again the very next day. Orders had come through for the LST flotilla, and Purdon's policy was to pass on important orders in person. There were sure to be questions he would have to answer.

When Purdon stepped from his gray-painted jeep onto the *1525*'s dock, the admiral found work still going on aboard the ship. A large crane was hosting a 112-foot tank landing craft, called an LCT, onto the main deck for transport overseas. A temporary super conning tower was also being erected to allow a signalman visibility over the piggy-backed landing craft. The rest of the *1525*'s equipage appeared to be in place. Some dozen 20mm guns lined her decks, and 40mm guns protruded from gun tubs fore and aft.

Purdon trudged up the gangway and took salutes from the rattled gangway officer and his enlisted-man assistant.

"Tell your captain Admiral Purdon is here to see him," he ordered. "He doesn't have to come up here. I'll see him in his cabin."

Ensign Williams stammered, "Aye aye, sir," and hurried all the way to Cadgett's cabin. Williams found Cadgett going over some paper work spread out before him on the small desk attached to the bulkhead.

"Admiral Purdon's here to see you, sir," Williams reported cheerfully.

Cadgett glanced up from his work.

"Tell the admiral I'll see him on deck in a few minutes."

"He wants to come down here, sir."

"Then tell him I'm here waiting on him," Cadgett answered.

Williams scurried to deliver the captain's reply.

Returning with Purdon, Williams did the admiral's knocking for him and quickly cleared out.

Cadgett rose from his seat and with a wave of his hand invited the admiral to take the empty chair beside his desk. Purdon sat, grunted, and gazed around the cabin. On the bookshelf were only the usual assortment of technical naval books found on every ship. If there was anything out of the ordinary in the cabin, it was a framed photograph turned face down on the desk.

"When an admiral takes the time to visit a lieutenant," Cadgett commented, "the news is either very good or very bad."

"Your ship's been detailed flagship of the flotilla," the admiral told him.

The expected smile provoked by the flattery of the appointment failed to appear on Cadgett's face.

"Somebody in Washington has faith in you," the admiral said.

"I don't know anyone in Washington, sir." Cadgett replied.

"I would think you'd be pleased. You are pleased, are you not?"

"To be truthful, sir, I'm not."

"You're not?"

Cadgett again did not answer.

"You have questions. Surely you have questions," Purdon demanded.

"No, sir, I don't."

"You're not curious about the ramifications?"

"I think I know what they are, sir," Cadgett said.

"Very well, I'll answer the questions you should ask. That is, if it is all right with you. It *is* all right with you, isn't it, Cadgett?"

"It is, sir."

"Good. Then let me proceed. The flag officer's name is Charles Bradford. By rank a captain. As flotilla commander he will bear the honorary title of commodore. He's an Academy man of the old school. From Boston, I think. He has a fine reputation and a good combat record. Like you, he spent the first couple of years of the war in the Pacific. While you were rising from ensign to lieutenant junior grade to lieutenant he was being promoted two steps up from lieutenant commander to captain.

"His aide," Purdon went on, "is a reserve lieutenant by name of Liam Fitzpatrick. One of those super smart types brought in by the war. At least that's what I'm told."

Cadgett's face showed disappointment.

Abruptly, Admiral Purdon pushed his chair back. The chair's metal legs scraped along the steel deck. The screech startled Cadgett; his head snapped up, and his eyes confronted the admiral's.

Admiral Purdon had seen Cadgett's personnel

jacket and he was not impressed. The Navy should not have commissioned him solely because he was born with a high IQ. Intelligence is nothing to boast about. It was a genetic accident, like the color of one's eyes. It was not sacrificed for or earned by hard work. Honesty, honor, loyalty, bravery, those were the measure of a man. They can't be taught in a few months of officer training. Men like Cadgett were unqualified by circumstance for admission to what had always been a gentlemen's club. War cheapens Navy life, Purdon believed.

Purdon had had enough of the man. He got up and strode angrily from the cabin.

***

"What are you doing in San Diego?" Admiral Zimmer asked when Cadgett appeared unexpectedly in his office. "Last I heard you were taking command of an LST in New Orleans."

"Got a ride from a pilot ferrying an SBD."

Zimmer moved his chair back, place his elbow on his desk, and used a loose fist to prop up his chin.

"Sit down and tell me," he said, "about those LSTs I've been hearing about."

Cadgett took a chair and leaned back, his eyes closed. He was tired. One does not sleep well in the gunner's seat of a dive bomber.

"It's just a big iron shoe box with bow doors for tanks to drive off a deck that looks like an underground garage," Cadgett explained wearily, and rubbed his knee at the site of a Pearl Harbor bruise. Seeing Zimmer again stimulated feelings that had their phantom effect.

"Powered?" Zimmer asked.

"Two GM V12-567 diesels, originally designed for railroad locomotives," Cadgett answered, and wrinkled his nose as if he had encountered something distasteful. "They'll push her to a blinding ten-and-a-half knots at flank speed. And they had to design her bottom so flat for beaching that she'll do thirteen-second rolls on a sea that's flatter than run-over cow

19

shit."

"Still, it's a command," argued Zimmer.

"Yeah, it's a command."

They fell silent for a moment. Despite the difference in their ranks, Cadgett was comfortable with Zimmer, as all men who had shared terrible events can be. Cadgett perceived that Zimmer envied him. He knew Zimmer was too young to be a rear admiral. His was a consolation prize. Cadgett had heard that Zimmer had managed to fool the Navy the first year and a half of the war, serving on a battleship in the Pacific until his disability became too obvious to ignore. He had reached the rank of captain by then, and, given the wounds he had suffered at Pearl Harbor, there was nothing the Navy could do but discharge Zimmer or promote him into a shore job.

"Yeah, it's a command," Cadgett repeated, "and they can have it."

Zimmer smiled tolerantly. He placed his palms together in an attitude of mock prayer and said, "Welcome to the U.S. Navy."

"Come on, Walter," Cadgett groused, annoyed at being patronized.

Zimmer leaned back and stared at the overhead.

"Do you know how many skippers are dissatisfied with their commands?"

Cadgett angled his head toward Zimmer.

"I need your help," he said hoarsely.

"Goddamn it, Verne, don't do this to me. You pulled me off the sinking ship at Pearl, and Lord knows I'm grateful. But I championed you for officer's training and wrote a reference for you that made you sound like Ferdinand Magellan. We're even, damn it!"

Cadgett lowered his voice to the point at which Zimmer had to strain to hear him. "You know where I'm from. So far back in the hills we had to wipe the owl shit off the clocks to see what time it was. I reckon my family's been in those hills near two hundred years, and for two hundred years we've been screwed by land speculators, by mine owners, by revenuers, by every two-bit son of a bitch in county, state, and federal government. They figured us for scum so they treated us like scum. I'm the first person in my family to graduate from high school, the first who can give orders instead of just take them. I just get my command, just get the meat in my mouth, and those gold-braided assholes in Washington designate my ship, my command, flagship of the flotilla."

"I see it as a big boost to your career," Zimmer tried.

"Now I'll tell you what I see." Cadgett responded, his voice rough with anger. "I see a flag officer aboard who outranks me. He'll have an aide with him who has the same rank I do. They'll be sitting in judgment of every decision I make, every order I give."

"You can deal with it, Verne."

"Let some other skipper have the honor of carrying the flotilla's flag or get me transferred to a different ship."

Zimmer's eyes shifted from Cadgett's face, pale from the conflict of anger and entreaty, to the back of his own hands.

"No, I can't, Verne," he murmured, his voice lowered to the pitch as Cadgett's. "It's too late. Your orders are cut."

"I don't believe it. You've got clout."

"You're over-reacting, Verne. As skipper, you'll be responsible for the ship and its crew. Bradford will have jurisdiction only over the flotilla as a whole."

"Technically," Cadgett answered, "but you and I both know in reality I'll be sucking hind tit."

"No more than anyone else in your position."

Cadgett's face went dark, and he spoke with an underlying tone of resentment. "Let me tell you something about my position. After the war, mustangs like me are going to be busted back to enlisted ranks or dropped off on the beach to manage Woolworth Five-and-Dimes. To beat the odds I'm going to have to show superior ability to command. This situation will make for doubt. They'll say, 'Sure he did well, but he had the old commodore to guide him every inch of the way.'"

Zimmer rolled his eyes upward and spread his palms. "Spare me, O Lord," he intoned.

"Get me out of this, Walter."

"Verne, you get yourself into the Navy chain of command or you know where you'll end up?"

"Yeah, I know where I'll end up. Back in Kentucky bore- sighting a mule's ass."

"I know you, Verne. You have a talent for carrying out orders. It's going to be all right." He paused. "Verne," he added sadly, "I'd give anything to be in your shoes."

***

Cadgett tried to get a flight back to New Orleans, but failed. The plane was either already filled, or it was a single seater, or the pilot didn't want company. All he could do was try to get a taxi to take him to Union Station. He failed in that, too. Every cab was booked. Cadgett ended up taking the naval station's bus to downtown San Diego. It was packed with sailors on liberty. Because Cadgett was an officer, the sailors did their best to provide him all the room they could spare. Even so, he was jammed in between a couple of seamen, who just days before had been posted to the base straight out of boot camp. They felt like airmen, but in truth they were as yet only drafted labor: hangar sweepers, airplane cleaners, box car unloaders.

There were other sailors on the bus, newly trained airmen awaiting assignment to aircraft carriers. They were thrilled at the prospect, speculating about which carrier they would be lucky enough to be assigned.

Cadgett wondered if he had ever been like them, all talk of pussy and tailor-made blues. He had taken the bus to Bowling Green and walked into the first storefront recruitment station in a line of three. It happened to be the Navy. It could have been the Marine Corps or the Army. It mattered little then. He had been determined to make a career out of it. He had nothing behind him but an unpainted shack, a dirty-faced little sister teasing a retired hound dog, a big sister pregnant by an unknown neighbor, a rickety father, a desiccated mother, a whiskey still hidden in the woods, and a dirt road in front that led only to the mines.

The train was another failure, number four for the day. There was nothing available but a coach seat. The train was an old one pressed back into service because of the war. The years had made it dirty in a way that no amount of cleaning could eradicate. The windows could not be forced open, the toilets would not flush and all that came from the water taps was a hissing sound.

Cadgett's next-seat companion was a pallid nun who neither smiled nor spoke, but remained ensconced in some long religious tract. She mouthed the words, nodding her black-wrapped head and sighing.

The train was only a short distance out of San Diego and the aisles were already strewn with used paper cups, crumpled cigarette packages and other detritus. The air was clouded with cigarette smoke and pungent with flatulence. Where the sailors on the bus had smelled of soap and talcum powder the train travelers smelled of sweat, spilled whiskey and Spearmint Chewing Gum.

Just before supper, the train's dining staff decided to refuse to work, protesting that they had taken all the abuse they could stand from returning Pacific war Marines.

By the time the train reached Tucson, some of the women had succumbed to the aphrodisiac of travel and paired off with servicemen in the darkened car under coats and blankets.

When the train finally limped into New Orleans, Cadgett welcomed the city as if it were New Jerusalem. Rumpled, hungry and unshaven, he hurried to the ferry that would take him across the Mississippi River to the Algiers Naval Station and his ship.

***

To Cadgett, mornings on a ship in port had an uncomfortable quality. Without the soothing sounds of the engines, he had slept fitfully and had lain awake in the steel silence of his room thinking over the situation in which he found himself. Without Zimmer's help he was doomed to skipper a ship overseen by an officer who could impede his career with a half-hearted compliment inserted into his personnel jacket. He at last realized, however, that he must play the cards he had been dealt: to "go along with the program," as they said.

Now Cadgett felt relieved, like a condemned man whose last appeal had been denied. There was a certain peace in being bereft of options, no matter how dire the consequences.

Cadgett swung from his bunk and hurried through his ablutions. When the steward's mate brought him his morning coffee, he told the man to have the yeoman report to him.

The yeoman, always known as "Pens," materialized almost immediately. It was a trick Cadgett always wondered about. How did he do it? Did he hang out just outside Cadgett's cabin twenty-four hours a day? The feat was really quite remarkable, and a little unnerving.

Pens was short and squat and almost bald, though not yet thirty. In civilian life he would be a bookkeeper or small businessman. His parents were immigrants from somewhere in the Balkans.

"Sometimes it's Macedonia and sometimes it's Bulgaria, and I think sometimes Greece," Pens would say. "I'm not sure where the place is now."

Pens was sent to yeoman school because he had scored high on that portion of the General Classification Test that measured clerical skills, and in this case the Navy got things just right. The man was a virtuoso on the typewriter.

Pens was so eager to please that Cadgett found giving him orders embarrassing.

"Tell the steward's mate I want lunch in my cabin at 1200 and all officers in the wardroom at 1400."

"Is there anything you want the colored boys to rustle you up special?"

"Pens, get your ass out of here."

Pens fled, and the captain returned to his paper work.

After lunch Cadgett napped for a while, then went up to the wardroom. He glimpsed Brown's head protruding into the passageway on alert for his arrival. As soon as Brown caught sight of Cadgett, in popped his head. As Cadgett stepped into the room Brown's voice shrilled, "Attention on deck!"

The officers stiffened until Cadgett waved "at ease." Still, some remained at partial attention.

This time Cadgett did not indulge in silence before speaking but moved right into what he wished to say.

"A," Cadgett said, incongruously holding up a single finger, "I don't like reserve officers."

One officer made a nervous gesture with his hand, another rubbed his forehead, and others breathed deeply. Some exchanged unhappy glances.

"B," Cadgett said, and holding up two fingers, "make a mistake and I'll read you off. Make the same mistake a second time and I'll kick you off."

"C," Cadgett went on, holding up three fingers, "the crew, they don't know asshole from tin cup. Neither do you. Even so, I'll hold each of you responsible for mistakes made by seamen in your respective divisions.

"D," Cadgett said, holding up four fingers, "officers are not permitted to cuss on my ship. Only I cuss on my ship."

"Liberty for the port section tonight. We sail Friday for a beaching exercise so don't tucker yourselves out honky tonkin', hear?"

At that, Cadgett turned and left as abruptly as he had entered.

The officers remained in their places.

"All right, you're dismissed," Brown announced.

"Honky tonkin'?" an officer commented slowly,

"What does he think we are, a bunch of pecker-woods?"

"Secure your spit locker, Mr. Butterly!" Brown ordered.

***

Instead of dispersing, the officers stood around silently staring past and above each other. After Brown left, they filed into the passageway and crowded into Lieutenant Craft's room. "What do you think, Chester?" Ensign Butterly asked.

"Some of these old salts can be cryptic," Craft answered, "You have to learn to interpret what they say."

"So you understand him?" asked Ensign Cornell.

"Not completely," Craft replied.

The officers frowned.

"But I will," Craft added.

"Let us know when you do understand the man. You can be our interpreter," Ensign Williams suggested sarcastically.

"Be your own damn interpreter," Craft refused.

"I say he's a Captain Bligh," Ensign McManus asserted.

"More like Captain Ahab," Williams said.

"Stop being so goddamn dramatic," Ensign Graves broke in.

"Goddamn? Goddamn? How dare you cuss on this ship?" Williams said. "Don't you know you risk being put on the Captain's *feces* list?"

***

Cadgett considered informing his officers of the appointment of their ship as flagship and the imminent arrival of the flag officer and his aide, but thought the better of it. They would interpret an announcement in that atmosphere as being of a great importance. That was the opposite of what he wanted. If he were to remain the one authority aboard, he needed to have them learn about Bradford's arrival as just another ordinary shipboard event. After supper that evening, Cadgett invited the officers to remain at table and drink a cup of coffee with him.

"By the way," Cadgett began in an off-handed manner, "in case you haven't heard, the *1525* will be flagship of the flotilla. The flag officer, Captain Bradford and his aide, Lieutenant Fitzpatrick, will be coming aboard probably sometime tomorrow."

"Are there any special preparations to make, Captain?" Brown asked.

"We can dispense with ceremony, Brown. Judging from our commissioning ceremony, short and sweet seems to be the fashion now."

"What berths do they get?"

Cadgett rubbed his nose while giving the question some thought.

"Ordinarily," he replied, "the flag officer would get the largest cabin. That's mine. However, don't move him in yet. My cabin is the only one on the ship with telephone communication to the wheelhouse. That could make for a problem."

"Very well, Captain. I'll stow their gear until I hear from you."

"Don't stow his aide's. Move him in with Graves. He has an empty bunk."

"Aye aye, sir."

"How do we address the flag officer, sir?" asked Williams.

"His rank is captain, but to avoid confusion he'll be addressed as Commodore. As for his aide, you can call him shit bird for all I care."

CHAPTER IV

"I feel like an intruder," Lieutenant Liam Fitz-patrick said, looking out the fog-clouded window of the hired car.

It was two days before Christmas, and in the Massachusetts countryside the snow lay in wind-driven drifts against the gray stone walls dividing farm from farm.

"You're being ridiculous," Commodore Charles Bradford snapped at him, "I spoke with my wife yesterday and she said she'd be glad to have you as a guest."

"Glad," Fitzpatrick thought, was a trifle weak. He would have preferred "delighted" or its equivalent.

Liam turned from watching snowed-under pastures along the road to the officer he had been assigned to assist. "Christmas is a family occasion. No time for strangers hanging around."

Bradford folded his arms on his chest and closed his eyes. He and Fitzpatrick were being driven down from Boston for three days leave before reporting for duty aboard the *1525* in New Orleans.

"Everything will be fine, you'll see," Bradford said.

Bradford was an unprepossessing man in his early 40's, of medium height, with milky blue eyes that seemed moist with sadness. His long, proud Puritan nose was the only feature that lent him a look of authority to go along with his captain's rank.

Dusk had descended when Bradford and Liam drove up the gravel driveway to the front door of the Bradford house. The driver, after helping them unload their luggage and accepting payment for the trip, wheeled the big '39 Packard around and sped off in a hail of cast-back stones.

The sound of the motor and the crunch of gravel under spinning tires brought the people in the house bursting out the front door.

Bradford's daughter Nora, home from Radcliffe College for the holidays, immediately started to pull off his coat.

"Welcome home, Dad," she cried. "We could hardly wait."

"Thank goodness you got here safely," June Bradford said. "The snow..."

"The roads are clear," Bradford reassures her. "The exhaust from all that holiday traffic dried them out."

"One wonders where they get the gas coupons to do all that driving," June mused.

"I'll make some sandwiches," Mildred, the Bradford's housekeeper interrupted, ever ready to anticipate the family's needs.

"Too close to supper. Just get us a Black Label," Bradford told her.

June turned to her husband's young aide, "I'm terrible sorry, Lieutenant, if we seemed to ignore you. We were carried away. I haven't seen my husband for months."

"Forgive us," Nora joined in. "We'll make it up to you with our hospitality."

"I understand," Liam protested weakly. "There's no need to apologize."

Still, Liam had to admit to himself that his premonition of feeling the outsider had materialized almost immediately upon his arrival.

Except for Mildred, who dashed off to fetch the drinks Bradford ordered, they all pitched in to drag the luggage into the foyer. June spread her arms out wide as if to embrace them all and herded them into the living room. She did not herself sit until they were all settled in the chairs scattered around the room.

June Bradford attached her eyes to Liam. She was looking at a big man with thick arms his uniform could not hide. The way his eyes moved and his head turned away from direct contact marked him as shy. His hair was as black as an undertaker's crepe and his skin was so white the veins coursing up the sides of his face were visible. He moved with an easy assurance, hiding his discomfort with an athlete's grace.

Liam had thrown himself into the chair with the words, "I'm sure glad to be here. That was one heck of a trip." Then he had run his fingers through his short hair and breathed a sigh.

"Mix me one too, while you're at it, Mildred," requested June.

June Bradford need not have bothered to ask. She already had four Scotches poured over ice in the Baccarat glasses that Bradford always said made drinks taste better.

"Cheers," said June, a small woman with tiny, coffee-colored eyes, touched-up hair, and an almost fleshless body. Her mouth was small and her nose beak-like. She was a fading beauty, a featherless bird who seemed always poised to peck away at someone's eyes. She sipped at her drink not once but twice.

"Yes, happy days," Liam toasted. "Thanks for inviting me. I hope I won't be a burden."

"We're glad you're here," June said with little conviction.

There was that word "glad" again, Liam thought, and gulped his drink. He gazed around the room. He wondered at the furnishings. Everything, it seemed, was a little shabby. The furniture was early American in style, though he couldn't tell whether it was authentic or reproductions. He supposed the family was well to do, even rich. If so, why was everything in such deplorable condition? Liam had glimpsed a five-year-old Chrysler station wagon, with unrepaired body damage and rusted rocker panels, parked off to the side of the house. Surely they could afford something newer. Liam watched Nora drink with practiced motions and wondered why the Bradford's accepted with equanimity the drinking of a college-aged daughter.

Liam supposed men found Nora Bradford attractive. She was dark-haired and blue-eyed, a fetching combination. Nora's crossed legs were shapely, if slightly muscular. Her nose was a replica's of her father's, only smaller, narrower and certainly elegant. Nora stared at Liam with clear, questioning eyes, noticing her interest, looked away to the paintings on the walls, portraits of 18th century men and women. Most were done in primitive styles that spoke of a Colonial heritage. Certainly the Bradford name was distinguished. Liam was almost on the mark. Oddly, Commodore Charles Winslow Bradford, despite being a descendent of William Bradford, did not come by the name by way of the celebrated Pilgrim governor of the Plymouth Bay Colony. The patronymic came down from a John Bradford who had come to the colony years later with the Puritans and was in no way related to the framer of the Mayflower Compact. Still, June Bradford was content to allow people to believe that they got their name from the governor. It lent more authenticity to aristocratic provenance. For the same reason, June Bradford had prevailed upon her husband to buy and refurbish an 18th century farm house less than a hour's drive from the site of the original colony. With its acquisition, the harmless deception was complete.

"Liam, What an odd name!" June commented.

"It's Irish for William. My father's Irish."

"Your accent, Lieutenant, are you from the Midwest?" June asked.

"No, ma'am, San Francisco."

"The city?"

"Yes, Pacific Heights."

June Bradford raised her chin, setting her eyes on the curtained windows behind Liam.

"I suppose it's hard to get around there. Like New York."

The words flowed from June lazily, as if she really did not care what the answer was going to be. It was just conversation.

Liam caught her disinterest, but answered with pleasant alacrity.

"No, we have an excellent public transportation system."

"You mean you ride buses?" Nora asked.

"Rarely. We keep a car. My dad couldn't do without his new Caddy every year."

"I see..." Mrs. Bradford said, her voice trailing off to silence.

"Come on, Liam, let's get up stairs and get cleaned up for supper," Bradford interrupted cheerfully.

"Aye aye, sir," Liam replied with a grin.

Liam was happy to disengage himself from Mrs. Bradford. The fact that he would be spending three days with her now struck him with some force. He was convinced that he had made a mistake in accepting Bradford's invitation, even if a refusal would have made him seem ungrateful.

Liam went to the foyer, got his luggage and followed Mildred up to a small bedroom. The room was obviously meant for a second servant, but it was comfortable enough.

After a shower and a second shave just to make sure there would be no hint of a beard, Liam joined his hosts downstairs where they spoke mostly of local history and the relative merits of thoroughbred horses. Nora revealed that she kept a horse named Sierra in a one-horse stable on the property and promised to introduce Liam to him the next day.

"I take it you're not horse people," June said.

32

"No. Scared to death of the beasts."

After a light supper of cold chicken, they again went into the sitting room where they proceeded to drink until they were too tired to remain awake. The Bradfords climbed the stairs without stumbling, and Liam got the idea that this was a regular ritual at the Bradford house. Liam, on the other hand, drank too much only on weekend binges when he had been at college, and on his occasional forays into the more disreputable bars of San Francisco.

***

Outside the Bradford house, the snow began to melt from the overnight arrival of mild winds from the southeast. In the fields, brown patches emerged from snow cover and meltwater dripped from daggers of ice hanging from the eaves of the house. While he dressed, Liam took in the view from his window that looked out the rear of the house toward the stable and the ganglia of branches on the bare trees beyond.

When Liam went down for breakfast he found Nora fresh and radiant in a pink angora sweater and a gray pleated skirt. Much to his embarrassment, she was staring just below his belt buckle. He had occasionally experienced that phenomenon in the past and it always made him uncomfortable, much as a woman experiences when she finds a man staring down the front of her dress.

"Morning, Nora," Liam greeted her, gazing around the room for the Bradfords.

Nora shifted her eyes to his face and said, "They're not down yet. Dad makes up for the lack of rest aboard ship by sleeping in at home."

The sound of conversation brought Mildred from the kitchen.

"Anything special for breakfast, Lieutenant?"

"Just orange juice and coffee".

"Coming up," Mildred said, and returned to the kitchen.

He watched Nora drinking her coffee and said, "Where's the tree?"

"Tree?"

"Christmas tree."

"Oh, we don't have a tree," Nora told him. "Never have."

Liam said nothing, and Nora filled the void with an explanation.

"Dad's folks believed Christmas celebrations were, I don't know, pagan or something. The attitude goes way back."

"I understand," Liam said, though he didn't understand at all.

"Oh, here they are," Nora exclaimed, seeing her parents coming down the stairs.

Liam whispered to Nora, "Is it all right if I wish them a Merry Christmas?"

She laughed. "Of course."

"Merry Christmas," Liam called to them.

Bradford replied, "Yes."

Saying that, he and June sat down at the table.

"Merry me no Christmases," June answered. "I am not prepared for the mawkishness of the season."

Liam recoiled.

"Don't mind mother, Liam, she's always grouchy this time of the day."

"It looks like it's going to be nice weather for Christmas Eve," said Liam, feeling them out, for he was confused about the demeanor he should adopt.

Mildred entered with their breakfasts and they began to eat in silence.

Finally Bradford spoke up.

"Mother and I will be going into town. We have some matters to attend to," he said directing his words to Nora.

"Go with God", Nora responded jocularly.

"I'm sure you two will find something to do while we're in town," June said, with an almost imperceptible smile.

"Sure we will," Nora agreed, biting off the corner of a slice of buttered toast.

Almost everything the Bradfords said had a sarcastic undertone to it, and Liam decided he'd best speak as little as possible for fear of becoming a target. He shook his head to present a neutral manner and gulped from a nearly empty coffee cup.

"You'll be entertained," June promised turning to Liam. "My daughter relates well to men. Indeed, she adores them. Just ask any male in Cambridge between the ages of 18 and 39."

"Forty-nine," corrected Nora. "There was a gentleman this past semester, a professor of philosophy, with whom I became great friends."

"Let's go," Bradford said, and with a display of annoyance threw his napkin on the table and stood up.

After the Bradfords had gone, Nora lingered over a cigarette and a third cup of coffee delivered by Mildred without prompting.

"You don't smoke?" Nora asked him.

"No. Never started."

"Surely you had some vices as a boy."

"Of course."

"Tell me about them?"

"Not a chance," Liam said.

"Oh, come on. Don't be a prig."

"No."

"You shoplifted from the five-and-ten-cent store."

"Not that I remember."

"You cheated on tests."

"I ain't talkin'."

"You spied on the lady next door while she undressed."

"There was no lady next door."

"You practiced onanism."

"What?"

"Flipped your stomach. Beat your meat. Whacked off."

"My God," Liam said, genuinely shocked. "What in the world do they teach you at a girls' college?"

Nora laughed aloud. "I'm just trying to get a rise out of you. Come along. I'll introduce you to the finest Palomino in this part of the country."

Liam followed her through the kitchen and out the back door into the shrinking patches of snow.

Nora took him by the hand and led the way.

"I know where the obstacles are," she said.

Liam felt her hand in his, warm and dry to the touch despite the cool, moist air.

When they approached the stable, Liam saw a tall man leave, pick up a pitchfork that was leaning against the outside wall, and go back into the stable.

"Somebody's in the stable," Liam said.

"That must be Ritter. One of our neighbors. Retired banker. Raises Black Angus cattle and keeps a few Arabians."

Liam found the going slow. It was hard to tell what lay just under the snow.

"A local boy comes to clean the stable once a week," Nora continued "and Ritter feeds Sierra while I'm at school. Comes over every day while I'm away."

"Nice of him."

"Oh, he's compensated all right," She muttered almost under her breath.

"Hello, Nora," said Ritter, young looking for his age and patently self-assured.

Nora did not return the greeting. Instead she proceeded to introduce the two men. It was a curt introduction.

"Walter Ritter, Lieutenant Liam Fitzpatrick."

"How do you do?" Ritter said, but did not offer to shake hands. He merely half-smiled, pushed his recently barbered brown hair from his forehead, then went to the other end of the stable and resumed preparing the horse's feed.

"And this, my friend, is my Sierra," Nora said putting her hands on either side of the horse's nose and rubbing vigorously. "Like him?"

"He looks nice. I don't know anything about horses."

She took one hand off the horse's nose and turned to Liam.

"How old are you, Liam?"

"Twenty-six."

"Never married, of course."

"Of course."

"I don't suppose you'd answer if I asked why."

"Shall I give you my funny answer to that question or my serious one?"

"Your funny one. It will be more accurate."

"I hold with the upper class Englishman who said, the pleasure is momentary, the position ridiculous and the expense abominable."

"I didn't ask you why you don't have sex, I asked why you never married."

Liam reddened. He was mortified. How had he made such a stupid mistake? Whatever was he thinking?

Ritter came by carrying a bucket of feed. When Nora noticed him she shot him a cold glance and said loud enough for him to hear, "Well I don't believe in marriage, either. I've been disillusioned by unkept marriage vows."

Ritter glanced at her, put the bucket down, and left the stable.

"I did not for one second believe you," Nora added, after Ritter was gone. Then she moved close to Liam.

"About what?"

"About what the Englishman said."

"It's just a joke."

"Prove it," Nora said and looked directly into Liam's eyes as she pressed her body hard against him.

He paled and pushed her away as gently as he could.

"What are you doing?" he asked, much surprised.

"Guess," she said reaching down and grabbing his buttocks with both hands.

Trying to lurch away from her, Liam slipped on the stable muck. Instinctively he reached for the wall to break his fall. It slowed him, but still he found himself on the ground. In his struggle to rise he did not at first feel her hand unbuttoning him. When he realized what was happening, he tried to shunt his body to one side, but by then her fingers had seized him just behind his glans. She pulled his flesh up toward her and, with an animal-quick downward thrust of her head, mouthed it. There was no possible response to the moist friction that enveloped it except the flow of blood. Now he was erect in her and he could do nothing but wait. All at once he stiffened.

Still on the stable floor, Liam leaned his back against the wall. He was not angry, he was just surprised that she gotten that response from him.

"Well?" Nora asked after a while.

"Let's go back to the house."

"Girl rapes man, that's news."

"Let's go back to the house," Liam repeated.

Now her small smile turned into a laugh and Liam interpreted it not of derision but of embarrassment. Not for her, but for him, for his timidity, his reluctance and his ludicrous surrender. His face flushed crimson.

"All right," Nora agreed. "Let's go back to the house."

***

Later, it was as if nothing had happened between them. Condemned to be together with Nora for the rest of the day and part of the next, there was nothing for Liam to do but pretend the incident never occurred. He invented a friendly rivalry. They played backgammon and when they tired of that, table tennis.

When the Bradfords returned from town, their arms sagging with bags of groceries, Liam and Nora joined them putting things away. Liam noticed there was one small package Mrs. Bradford kept close to herself. By then it was late afternoon, and while Mildred was busy preparing dinner, the Bradfords and Liam returned to their rooms to dress.

Darkness had fallen when Liam, looking fresh and military in his dress blue uniform, came down to join the Bradfords. On his breast he wore the American Theater of Operations ribbon, the only campaign medal to which he was entitled. Bradford's chest, on the other hand, was stacked with three tiers of ribbons denoting a multitude of campaigns and awards.

In light of Liam's conversation with Nora about how little value the Bradfords placed on Christmas celebrations, he had reconciled himself to an ordinary dinner and a prosaic holiday. He was surprised when Mildred entered the dining room carrying a huge roasted turkey on a silver platter. Looking delighted with her handiwork, Mildred placed the turkey before Commodore Bradford and turning her head, winked at Liam.

"Special for you, Lieutenant," Nora said, stood up and performed a mock bow accompanied by the pleasant rustling of her taffeta dress.

June unsmilingly pushed the small, plainly wrapped package toward Liam. He stared at it, not sure what to do.

"Open it," Bradford insisted.

"It's for you, Liam," Nora told him.

June Bradford, quite patrician in a black velvet dress and pearls watched with a look of boredom on her face as Liam picked up the unexpected offering. He removed the outer wrapping, trying not to tear it, and opened the box to find a white silk scarf.

"Don't know what to say," Liam stumbled. "I have no gifts for any of you. Orders from the Commodore."

"That's all right," June said, shaking her head from side to side, "when something's offered, grab it." Then she laughed and fingered her pearls.

Liam notice that Bradford cast a reproving glance at his wife, then turned to Liam and smiled.

"Before we demolish this—this thing here, I will, in honor of our young guest, sing a ditty our dear departed uncle St. John Palmer used to sing every Christmas when he was in his cups.

"And he had a plenitude of cups," Nora said.

"Speak well of the departed, dear," instructed June.

Bradford lifted his glass and proceeded to sing.

> I am Jesus little lamb
> Yes, by Jesus Christ I am.

"Dad," Nora said, "Liam doesn't know Uncle St. John's song was a joke. Perhaps he's offended."

"Nonsense," June countered, "of course he isn't."

"I admit it did make me a bit uncomfortable", Liam said.

"You take your religion seriously, don't you?" June asked.

"Yes, I do".

"What's your new ship like, Dad?" Nora said, changing the subject.

"It's one of those new tank landing ships. Transports eighteen Sherman tanks. Takes them right up onto the beach. A crew of a hundred or so. Not very glamorous compared to the duty I've had in the Pacific."

"Have you met the skipper?"

"No, I haven't. Don't know much about him except that his name's Cadgett. A mustang. Up from the ranks. He served on a cruiser in the Pacific the first years of the war. Heard anything about him, Liam?"

"Only that he's considered a first rate seaman and he was awarded the Silver Star for heroism during the Pearl Harbor attack."

"Sounds like a good man," Bradford observed.

"At this very moment he's plotting against you," said June.

The remark brought Liam's head around and Bradford frowned.

"Don't say that, June, you don't even know the man."

"Don't have to. No skipper likes a flag officer aboard. Makes them nervous."

"Let's go at the bird." Bradford made a cutting motion with his hand.

Bradford picked up a fork and a carving knife, then sliced off thick slabs of white meat and left them on the platter. "Serve them, will you, Mildred?"

Mildred came to attention, forked a slab of turkey onto the dinner plates and served them each in turn. On Liam's plate she laid two generous slices, one atop the other.

"Too much," Liam protested.

"Eat it all, Lieutenant," Mildred insisted. "You'll need your strength to whip those Japs."

"We must all obey her, Liam, or she'll take a job in a war plant and make some real money," joked Nora.

"Not a chance," Mildred replied. "If I wanted to do a man's work I'd have stayed in Poland."

***

June Bradford got out of bed, shimmied her body back into her nightgown and poured herself a drink from a bottle of Scotch stashed in the dresser.

Bradford said, "No, June, you've had enough."

"You're right," she agreed.

June poured the whisky in her water glass into the sink, rinsed her glass, filled it with water from the pitcher on her night stand, and climbed back into bed.

Outside their bedroom, the moonlight behind nearby trees cast shadows of twisted branches through the window, creating grotesque shapes on the wall of their room.

"Did you have to bring that boy home with you?" June asked.

The question did not surprise Bradford. He had been expecting an attack on the young man since the moment June objected to his visit. He turned on his side and stared at his wife.

"He's my aide. I couldn't leave him to wander the cold streets of Boston during Christmas while I'm home with my family enjoying the 'mawkishness of the season,' as you put it."

June stared at the shadows on the wall.

She answered without looking at him. "He has a home. He could have gone home."

Suddenly aware of a draft sweeping over his body, Bradford pulled the blanket up to cover the bottom half of his naked body.

"June, the boy's from San Francisco. Even if he could get a flight there and back there isn't enough

41

time."

"A merry Christmas for junior officers isn't your responsibility. Do you want me to sing Christmas carols under his window tonight?"

"Oh, for God's sake," Bradford said and pulled the blanket up to his neck.

"I don't like the way Nora looks at him".

"So that's it!"

"Yes, that's it," June said, turning to confront him, her eyes shining with malevolence.

"June, I know that young man. He's a religious Catholic. The next thing to being a priest. He's obsessed with religion. He goes to church as often as he can. He reads nothing but religious books. Catholic things."

"I don't know. Are you sure he is not concealing a lump in his underwear?"

"She could do worse," Bradford commented idly.

"What?"

June was sitting up now. "She could do *better*. A hell of a lot better. Didn't you hear him? '*A new Caddy every year*.' I'll bet they have wall-to-wall carpeting, and a Picasso etching on the wall they don't even know is a phony. Is that *us*?"

"June, please...."

"What's his father do...drive a taxi?"

"As a matter of fact he's a rather well-respected politician."

"An Irish politician. Cigars. Beer. Spitoons. Thank goodness he's leaving tomorrow." June rolled over on her back again and resumed watching the shadows on the wall.

"I know you're fed up with me, disgusted," she went on. "I'm beginning to shrivel. Look at my breasts. The life's going out of them."

"I'm no Adonis."

"In your uniform you still cut a dashing figure. And your love-making. You can still do the job."

"Well, thank you very much indeed."

June stopped talking. A breeze shook the tree branches outside their window and the shadows on the wall reconfigured themselves into unidentifiable

42

shapes.

"It's dangerous out there," Nora said in a voice too loud for the moment.

"What?" Bradford replied, startled by her tone.

Nora turned on her side and looked at him silently for a time.

Finally, she said, "If you find a desirable Miss overseas, deny everything when I question you."

"Me cheat?" Bradford said jocularly.

"No, seriously," Nora said.

"You're really inviting me to lie to you?"

"Lies are the gravity of love, Charles, they permit us to orbit around each other without colliding."

"Ah, yes," Bradford said sadly. "You shall admit the truth and the truth will wreck your life."

Bradford suddenly rolled over onto June and roughly lifted her nightgown. Afterwards, exhausted, he lay down beside her, breathing hard.

"It's exciting when you're impatient that way," June told him, her cheeks burning.

"I wanted to tend to business while the urge was still there."

"You're rather good at business. I've always told you that."

"You know sailors," he kidded. "Animals are what we are."

Suddenly, she said, "Charles, I want to save this marriage."

"So do I," he agreed.

"It won't survive unless we build a stable family life. Time is running out."

"That means I quit the Navy and start mowing the lawn."

"I'm serious, Charles. People wouldn't understand if I left you while you're away at war. But if you don't resign the moment the war ends, our marriage ends."

"I can't quit, June. There is no life for me outside of the Navy. I would wind up resentful, and you would be even more unhappy."

"That's it?" she demanded.

43

"I can't leave the Navy, June. I can't."

"You're being awfully calm about it."

"I've expected it for a long time," he admitted.

***

The next day, after lunch, they all set out for Boston in the Chrysler station wagon. A cold front from the north had driven away the mild winds of the day before and the snow had frozen in place. The meltwater on the roadway became thin panes of ice that continued for long stretches before the black of the highway showed through.

When they arrived in Boston, they stopped only to turn in their last ration coupons for gasoline. Bradford parked near the train station and they stood on the platform together as the porters loaded the hand carts with the men's luggage. Soon, the Bradfords separated from Nora and Liam and stood off where they could not be overheard.

June put her head on her husband's shoulder. It was a rare show of affection, and Bradford felt an old tenderness for her well up inside of him. He knew June had a horror of any display of emotion in public, and he thought perhaps she expected never to see him again.

"Charles..."

"Yes?"

"I've had twenty years of these goodbyes. I'm sick of them."

"June...."

"Goodness knows, we don't need the extra pension money ten more years' service will provide us."

Bradford gently pushed her head up off his shoulders and stared into her eyes.

"I was a sailor when you married me, and I want to continue being a sailor as long as they let me."

June answered, "You never had to be, Charles. Your father begged you to come work with him. You would do very well. You have a good head for it. Look how well our investments have done."

"You want me to sell bonds? I'd rather open my veins."

"You want to be a sailor," she said, "but do they want you anymore? Sure they need you now because of the war. But for what? To take over a flotilla of LSTs? Landing ships, for heaven's sake—landing ships! Not cruisers or destroyers, not fighting ships. Charles, they're telling you something. Read the Navy's moves, not its words."

Bradford was stung by his wife's argument. His chin dropped almost imperceptibly. He no longer wanted to talk about it. He turned his attention to his daughter standing with his aide just out of earshot. He watched her alternately try to intimidate, then charm Liam. Having a child is playing dice with genes, he thought. Still, he loved her and it pained him to think how she would react when and if they received that telegram starting, "The Secretary of the Navy regrets to inform you..."

**

Nora said, "I think I hear your train, Liam."

"Well, World War II, here I come."

"Write to me, will you?"

Liam paused and looked searchingly into her eyes. "About what? The sea? The sky? Shipboard routine? You know all about that stuff already."

Nora shrugged. "All right. I'll pretend you don't write because you're too busy."

"That's okay. Think that."

"Do you mind telling me why you don't want to write?

"It's just better that way."

CHAPTER V

"That's it?" Liam said, gazed up at the ship tied to the dock. The look on his face was unmistakable. He was disappointed with what he saw.

"That's it," Bradford answered and smiled.

"It looks like a—a stackless tanker".

Standing at the foot of the gangway, Liam looked around for the greeting party. All he could see at the on the ship's deck was a lone sailor in undress blues wearing a web belt and a holstered .45 semi-automatic pistol.

"Hey, sailor!" Liam shouted up to him, "How about getting us some help with this gear?"

"Sorry, sir," the man replied, "the crew's at chow, on liberty or on watch."

Liam was not pleased. He turned to Bradford. There was anger in his voice. "Cadgett had plenty of time to make arrangements for your arrival."

"Don't let it bother you, Liam. It's probably just an oversight."

"Damn it, Commodore, it's part of his job to be prepared for your coming aboard."

"Cadgett didn't rise from apprentice seaman to command of a United States naval vessel by neglecting his duty," Bradford replied.

Liam frowned. "I think it's a deliberate insult."

"It may be just that another rooster's been thrown into his barnyard," Bradford said.

"What then? A cockfight?"

"Don't worry, Liam, I'll do my best to keep the feathers from flying."

"Well, I suppose we'll know soon enough," Liam said and glanced despairingly at their luggage on the dock. "Wait here, sir, I'll get my gear aboard and come back for yours."

"Don't bother," Bradford refused. "I can use the exercise."

It took them two trips to get the luggage on the deck, Liam's anger growing by the minute.

"Where's the gangway officer, son?" Bradford asked the sailor.

It was the first time Liam had heard Bradford address an enlisted man. His tone was kindly and un-threatening, more like a solicitous clergyman speaking to one of his parishioners than a high ranking naval officer talking to a seaman.

"He went to the head, sir," the sailor stammered, frightened by the "scrambled eggs" on the visor of Bradford's cap.

"All right, son, Lieutenant Fitzpatrick and I will go up to the wardroom. When the gangway officer gets back, tell him Commodore Bradford's aboard. He is to stow our gear in a temporary place that the lieutenant and I can use until Captain Cadgett assigns us our billets."

"Aye aye, sir," the seaman said.

After a wrong turn in officer country, Liam and Bradford found their way to the wardroom where they sat down and waited. It wasn't long before Lieutenant Brown showed up, followed by two sailors carrying Liam and Bradford's luggage.

"Sorry we weren't standing by for you," Brown apologized with a hint of insincerity. "We're remiss on the hotel service, sir. You might say we're just too busy getting ready to fight a war."

"And you are?" Bradford questioned.

"Lieutenant Brown, sir, executive officer."

"And where is Captain Cadgett?"

"Ashore, sir. Taking care of ship's business. He'll be back in time for chow, sir. Suppose I find you a place where you can rest up before dinner."

"Good idea, Brown," Bradford agreed. "Let's do it."

"Aye aye, sir. I'll take care of it, sir," Brown said.

Turning to the two sailors who brought the luggage, Brown ordered, "Take the gear down to Graves' cabin. The commodore and the lieutenant will follow you. Okay, turn to!"

***

Cadgett materialized in front of Bradford and Liam without warning.

"I'm Cadgett."

He did not look at Liam or acknowledge his presence.

"Oh, yes-Cad-Cadgett-yes," Bradford stammered.

If Cadgett was pleased or amused at having put a superior officer at a disadvantage, he didn't show it. "We can go over all the official stuff later. Let's chow down first. I'll see you in the wardroom."

Recovering, Bradford said, "Yes, glad to meet you, Captain. We'll be up directly. After supper will be fine for the official matters. This is my aide, Lieutenant Liam Fitzpatrick."

Cadgett didn't speak. He merely nodded at Liam, then turned and left.

"What was that about?" Liam asked.

"What?" asked Bradford.

"Rude, is what I'd call it," Liam answered.

"Well, he certainly has a different style," Bradford said. "Let's go to supper."

Seated around the mess table, the LST *1525*'s officers started to rise when Bradford and Liam entered, but Cadgett waved them to remain seated.

"The mess is no place for ceremony," he commented, and added, "Men, Commodore Charles Bradford, flotilla commander." He went on to introduce the officers, calling each by name and rank. Cadgett overlooked introducing Liam.

"And this is my aide, Lieutenant Liam Fitzpatrick," Bradford put in after Cadgett finished introducing the officers.

The officers nodded a mild greeting.

Two stewards' mates rushed in with chairs for the newcomers.

As the soup was being served, Cadgett said, "Sorry, Commodore, but there's no room on an LST for a senior officers' mess. If you prefer, I can have you served separately. That is, if you don't mind eating alone."

"No need for that. I prefer this. It gives me the opportunity to get to know every one of you."

Cadgett attacked his bean soup with gusto.

"We're just a mustang skipper and a few raw ninety day wonders," Cadgett said between spoonfuls. "There isn't an Annapolis man among us. Not a one."

"Some of the finest officers I've known did not attend the Academy," Bradford pointed out.

Some of the crew's officers looked down at their soup. Brown smiled a small smile.

Cadgett looked at Fitzpatrick. "You Annapolis, too?"

"Notre Dame," Liam answered.

"Liam Fitzpatrick?" Cadgett questioned, raised his head and closed his eyes, thinking. "Liam Fitzpatrick? Are you the Liam Fitzpatrick who dropped the pass that lost the big game for the Irish a few years back?"

"The same. Not my proudest moment."

"Well, Lieutenant, I hope you don't drop the ball on this ship. This is one game we can't afford to lose."

"If I do, I'm sure you'll be the first to notice, Captain."

"Say, Lieutenant," Brown asked, "the priests at Notre Dame. Is it true they do funny things to themselves while listening to confession about sins of the flesh?"

"Only when they become bored with pederasty, Mr. Brown," Liam answered.

"Pederasty, eh?" Cadgett said.

"It means..."

"I know what it means, Lieutenant," Cadgett answered petulantly.

Cadgett pushed his soup bowl away. "That was pretty good soup, wasn't it, men?" The officers nodded.

"I understand you were stationed in Washington, Commodore," Cadgett said.

"Yes", Bradford answered.

"Did you have the honor of meeting Admiral King?"

"Yes, Captain, I did. Twice."

"Did you meet the President?"

"No."

"How about Eleanor?" Brown asked.

"Eleanor?"

"Roosevelt."

"Matter of fact, I did once," Bradford said. "At a Navy Day reception."

"Have you heard the rumor that she's a dyke?" Brown asked.

"A what?" Bradford said.

"A dyke," Brown said. "Mr. Fitzpatrick knows what a dyke is, don't you, Lieutenant? Notre Dame has provided Mr. Fitzpatrick with an excellent vocabulary."

Liam answered Brown slowly. His normally ruddy face was now aflame, his teeth clenched, the corners of his mouth tight. "I know," he agreed.

Bradford said, "I must say I haven't a clue to what that means."

Brown leaned back in his chair, folded his hands on his lap and spoke, *"Haven't a clue?"* He paused, then went on, "By your leave, Commodore, we follow a rule they have on some ships that call at English ports. Anyone who uses Brit talk is fined ten dollars to go toward financing a shore party. Of course, you and Mr. Fitzpatrick are exempt. Not formally part of the ship's company, you can talk as Limey as you like. It won't cost you—a farthing."

Bradford laid a hand on Liam's knee. He squeezed, then shook his head. Restrained, Liam took a breath and cocked his head. "A shore party! How perfectly marvelous. If there's going to be a poetry recital I do hope you'll invite me, Mr. Brown."

Cadgett grinned. He closed one eye and leaned toward Liam."Mr. Fitzpatrick, that sounds like something a pogue would say."

"Really, Captain?" Liam answered.

"Hey, mates," Brown interjected, "I heard a good one ashore. It seems these two colored soldiers see a plane heading right for them. The first says, 'Wud kinda plane id dat?' The other answers, 'Dats a B-2.' 'Wud kinda plane is a B-2?' the first soldier asks. The second soldier says, 'B-2 goddamn bad if it ain't one of ours.'"

Brown laughed aloud. It was as if he had heard the joke rather than told it. The two black stewards who overheard Brown's joke while serving, glanced at Brown as disdainfully as they dared. While Cadgett laughed, the other officers only smiled thinly. Bradford and Fitzpatrick remained stone-faced.

"I think the crew can use a little more practice, Captain," Cornell interrupted. "They were late answering the General Quarters drill this morning."

"Mr. Cornell," Cadgett began, ticking off his admonishments with his fingers. "A, you will not discuss ship's business at mess. B, you will not address me first unless it involves the safety of this ship. C, from what Mr. Brown tells me about your proficiency as an officer, you couldn't organize a pissing contest in a brewery."

Blood rushed to Cornell's face. He swallowed hard and the tears that watered over his eyes came just short of falling on his cheeks. "I'm sorry, sir," he squeaked.

Bradford abruptly changed the subject. "When will you be moving out of your cabin, Captain? I'd like to get settled."

"I know the rules call for you to get the largest quarters but I would like to make an exception in this case."

"Really, Captain? Why?"

"On an LST, the Captain's cabin is the only one with communication directly to the wheelhouse. If you take my cabin, the Officer of the Deck will have to send a messenger below to get me if he needs me."

Bradford looked up at the overhead before replying.

"I wish it could be otherwise, Captain, but I think we're obliged to follow the rules."

Cadgett's eyes darted around the wardroom. The officers cringed. Cadgett's attention finally fell on his food.

"Steward!" he shouted with deflected anger, "This meat is as thin as piss on a rock. You tell the cook if the book calls for it to be cut this thin I will be served double portions, hear?"

"And Mr. Fitzpatrick of Notre Dame fame should always gets double portions of potatoes," Brown added.

"Aye aye, sir," the steward acknowledged and got quickly out of Cadgett's sight.

"I'm hungry enough to eat the anus out of a dead nigra," Brown said. He smiled and added, "Notice, I did not use the vulgar anatomical term."

***

The day began as did every day aboard the LST *1525*. In accordance with Captain Cadgett's standing order, the song "Oh, What a Beautiful Morning" came crackling over the P.A. system. However, instead of it being followed by "Merzy Doats," as he prescribed, the voice of Chief, the ship's chief boatswain's mate, intruded into every corner of the vessel.

"Now hear this. Now hear this," he said. This was followed by the words that always focus a crew's attention, "This is the Captain speaking." Cadgett paused for a moment, then said, "We sail today for a beaching exercise in the Gulf. There are subs out there. I am now strapping on a .45. I'll wear it whenever we're in a combat zone. It is not for the enemy. It is for you. You whose finger freezes on the trigger. You who ducks when an enemy plane attacks. You who panics when we're hit by enemy fire. You who tries to abandon ship before it's ordered. I will shoot you *dead*. Without court martial. Without ceremony. Without mercy. Set Special Sea Detail. Prepare to get under way."

Liam Fitzpatrick could not believe that he heard right. Did Captain Cadgett really say he would execute crewmen out of hand? He was horrified. His status, though, prevented him from voicing his concern to the captain. Instead, he approached Bradford. He found him seated at the desk in the captain's former cabin, pages of dispatches spread out in a line before him, one atop the other, like huge playing cards in a game of giant solitaire. One elbow was on the desk and his chin was in his hand. His face was livid and he was staring at the bulkhead as if in a trance.

"Come on in, Liam," Bradford mumbled even though Liam was already in the cabin.

"You heard Cadgett's announcement, sir?" Liam asked.

"Yes," Bradford replied, still in agitated thought.

"It's outside the pale, isn't it, Commodore?" he queried, trying to keep his voice controlled so that he did not sound as if he were overstepping his rank.

Bradford lifted his chin from his hand.

"Yes, it is," he said.

"What happens now, sir?" Liam asked.

"I hate to stir things up, but I have no choice. Damn it, I was hoping for a smooth working relationship with the man."

"I feel better now that I know you're on top of it, sir."

"I wish I weren't," Bradford admitted.

***

Bradford roused himself from his chair and slowly set out through the passageway for the short walk to the captain's new billet. Unlike Cadgett's former cabin, it was divided from the passageway by a curtain instead of a door.

"Captain, are you there?" he called almost gently

at the curtain.

"I am," came Cadgett's voice.

"We have to talk."

"Come on in," Bradford heard Cadgett say after a few moments delay.

Bradford parted the curtain and entered the tiny room.

Cadgett was sitting up in his bunk, his back supported by a large non-regulation pillow. Open on his lap was a book on celestial navigation. On a nearby table was the day's decoded messages and a framed photograph lying face down.

Cadgett swung his legs over the side of the bunk and pulled himself up. Bradford sensed defiance in his body movement. To lower the temperature, Bradford reached toward the table to right the photograph.

"It must have fallen," Bradford pointed out.

"Don't touch that!" Cadgett cried.

Bradford pulled his hand back as if it had touched a flame. He found himself looking at the distorted features of a furious man.

"Sorry," Bradford said, but he didn't know what he had done to apologize for.

Bradford drew a deep breath. To remonstrate with Cadgett about the rudeness of his shout was one too many challenges for one day. He decided to ignore the captain's angry cry.

"I have a question about your announcement," he offered instead.

"Which one, sir?" Cadgett asked.

"Your most recent one."

"What about it?" Cadgett said, then added a belated "sir."

Bradford measured his words carefully. "I know you said those things to get the crew's attention. Don't you think they were too strong, even though you didn't mean them?"

"But I did mean them, sir," Cadgett answered.

"Come on, Captain. You're not going to shoot anyone."

"Commodore, this is not the First World War,

where it was just about won when we got into it. So far the bad guys are winning. Because of iron discipline. The Germans have it. The Japs have it. The French have lost it. The Brits are losing it. We've got to get it."

"There's some truth in what you say, Captain, but your solution is another matter. It's absurd. It could not survive a Navy inquiry. And Congress? I don't even want to think about it. Captain, please assure me that you will shoot no one."

Cadgett's jaw tilted toward Bradford in a posture of defiance.

Bradford stared back. The corners of his mouth were drawn so tightly that his lips were a thin blue cord above his jaw. Their eyes stayed locked for several long moments. Suddenly Cadgett's eyes relaxed. His eyelids dropped almost imperceptibly. His mouth slackened slightly.

"All right," Cadgett concurred, "but I'll still wear the .45. You can't stop me from that."

***

Though Cadgett said nothing about it, he could have predicted the positive results of his notorious announcement. Despite the outrage felt by Liam and the deep concern expressed by Bradford, the crew was to react in ways unexpected by both of them. If Bradford and Liam thought the men would be fearful or resentful, they were mistaken. Cadgett's announcement had the effect of energizing the crew. They now thought of themselves as the tough commanded by the tough, an elite kill-or-be-killed crew. Hereafter, they would go about their duties with renewed vigor. Every task, no matter how trivial, was now attacked with previously unknown enthusiasm. Orders would be responded to with a quicker step, their hearts having expanded with pride.

This new attitude, however, would pass unnoticed by Lieutenant Fitzpatrick and Commodore Bradford, who remained mostly below decks consumed by their duties. Liam stayed busy decoding and passing on to Bradford messages from the Navy Department and other points of origin, which Bradford turned them into orders for the flotilla. But when the *1525* cast off her lines and moved away from the dock and into the Mississippi River's navigation channel, there was an improved, if not expert, crew manning her.

***

The *1525* proceeded flawlessly from the Mississippi Delta into the Gulf of Mexico, en route to the Florida Panhandle.

The Navy, in its wisdom, had trained each of its raw sailors to perform one simple task. Coordinated by a few veterans, a highly complex operation unfolded smoothly.

The Gulf was green and gorgeous and as tranquil as a sea ever gets. Those in the crew who had never seen an ocean before were awed by the beauty of it and stunned by its expanse.

Approaching the shore for its beaching exercise, the *1525* was harried by gangs of delinquent dolphins that stole free rides on the waves nosed up by the ship's bow. The sweeping upward curve of their mouths gave them a look of permanent joy as they headed full speed at the ship, then veered off just before colliding with her hull.

"Sharks!" the young sailors cried when they saw the dolphins' dorsal fins cut through the water.

"Those are dolphins," Chief corrected them. "Now get back to work."

On the conn, above the wheelhouse, Liam, Bradford, Cadgett, and Brown, warmed by a pale, yellow sun shining down unhindered by clouds, watched the beach slowly loom closer.

"Lovely, isn't it?" Liam noted, unable to repress his delight at the sight of the white sand ahead stretching up to a wall of semi-tropical foliage.

"Lovely!" Brown repeated mockingly.

His response drew a questioning glance from

Bradford. Liam pretended not to have heard.

"Suggest steady as she goes," said Brown.

"Steady as she goes," Cadgett repeated to the Captain's talker who was on the phone to the Officer of the Deck in the wheelhouse.

"Steady as she goes," the OOD called, relaying the Captain's order to the quartermaster on the helm.

"Steady as she goes, sir," the quartermaster acknowledged.

"Suggest all ahead standard," Brown went on.

"All ahead standard," Cadgett said to his talker, who relayed the message to the OOD.

"All ahead standard," the OOD commanded the seaman on the engine order telegraph.

The sailor repeated the instruction as he pulled the annunciator levers moving the arrow to standard speed.

With his eyes galvanized to a single spot on the beach, Bradford addressed Cadgett.

"Captain, order flank speed."

"Pardon me?"

"Flank speed," Bradford repeated.

"That could damage our hull."

"Captain," Bradford reproved tolerantly, "we have to know how a ship built in a cornfield shipyard on the Ohio River will stand up to beaching at maximum speed."

"It's a little dangerous," Brown protested.

Bradford turned and stared coldly at Brown.

Brown reddened and almost seemed to physically shrivel under the commodore's gaze. His eyes darted from Bradford to Cadgett and back again, his tongue licked furiously at his lips.

Cadgett's face stiffened. His words came slowly, as if he wanted no misunderstanding about what he was about to say.

"Commodore, I think your order is unwise. We could knock this ship out of operation for days. We have an overseas schedule to meet."

Bradford heard him out, but would not be detracted from his goal. "Captain, it would be embarrassing if I had to tell my superiors why I could not give them the information they asked for."

"Captain, it's only that—," Liam started to say.

"Listen here, yardbird," Cadgett yelled at Liam. "Don't presume to give me orders on my own ship or I'll confine you below decks quicker than a cat can lick its ass, hear?"

"Do it, Captain. Flank speed," Bradford said more as a command than a request.

"Very well, Commodore. I will give the order, but I do it under protest, and Mr. Brown is witness."

Turning to the now petrified captain's talker, Cadgett ordered, "All ahead flank!"

"All ahead flank," the talker conveyed to the OOD.

"All ahead flank," said the OOD to the sailor on the annunciator.

"Flank speed, sir," the sailor replied and pulled the levers that turned the arrow that relayed the Captain's orders to the engine room.

After the stern anchor was dropped and the *1525*'s prow pushed onto the beach, there was a gentle bump, but nothing more. On some parts of the ship the movement of its bow up and onto the sand was not even felt.

The opportunity to gloat appeared to be ignored by Bradford and Liam, neither was there any acknowledgment by Cadgett and Brown of their having been overly cautious.

Cadgett ordered the bow doors opened and the ramp lowered—the steel apron tanks would use to roll onto the beach. Everything worked without a hitch and Cadgett was pleased that he would not have to return to New Orleans for repairs or adjustment of malfunctioning equipment. The LST retracted from the beach and stood out to sea where it rendezvoused with an airplane towing a target sleeve. The ship's 20mm and 40mm anti-aircraft guns banged away at the sleeve for an hour.

Cadgett was satisfied with the performance of the gun crews, considering that most had never fired a gun before, and certainly not at a target moving through the air.

That night, with the vessel lying anchored off Panama City, half the crew was allowed liberty. Most of the officers went ashore as well, and only Cadgett, Fitzpatrick, Bradford, and the crewmen on watch remained awake. All was dark and silent aboard the *1525*, and even the men on watch in the warm night drowsed standing at their stations. It would stay quiet like that until just before midnight when the liberty party would return.

CHAPTER VI

There's not a damn thing to do in this shit-kicking, redneck town," Chopcock complained.

Pulling Dago with him, he sat down on the curb. An 18-year-old signalman striker, Chopcock was narrow shouldered and had a waist so thin it looked as if a big man could envelop it with his hands. It was not only genetic; he found Navy food virtually inedible.

"It ain't New Orleans," Dago agreed.

Their liberty from LST *1525* was nearly over and they were eager for something to do, anything that differed from shipboard routine.

Like Chopcock, Dago was a city man raised in a Boston neighborhood populated by immigrants from a variety of backward countries. Built like a gladiator, he had a massive torso, short legs, and thick arms.

"Let's ask a cabby where the action is," Chopcock suggested. "Those guys know where things are happening."

Dago recognized the wisdom of his shipmate's words.

"Let's do it," said Dago and stood up, adjusted his white cap to an extreme tilt on the back of his head, and sallied into the road. He dodged a score or so of cars until a taxi came into view.

"Where can I take you, sailor?" the cab driver inquired in a deep Southern accent that was barely intelligible to the former petty thief and Mafia mascot.

"Where the action is."

"Maybe I can help," the cab driver said.

"Hey, Chopcock, we got a live one," Dago shouted.

Chopcock leaped to his feet and walked briskly to the middle of the road. The cab driver had never seen the likes of the two Yankees. They spoke a kind of English all right, but one looked like a foreign wrestler and the other had the sallow face of a dissipated jazz musician.

"You guys like to see a show?" the cab driver asked.

"You got to be kidding," Dago cried, throwing his hands up.

"No shows," Chopcock added, making a thumbs down motion.

"Not *that* kind of show," the cab driver refuted, then took his hand off the wheel, rested his left arm on the top of the door and lowered his voice conspiratorially. "For five bucks I can take you to see something y'all never seen before."

"Yeah, like what?" asked Chopcock cynically.

The cab driver smiled a lascivious smile and rolled his eyes heavenward.

"A woman and donkey," he whispered.

"A woman and a donkey?" Dago exclaimed. "What the hell's that?"

"I know what he means," Chopcock said. "Yeah, we'll go for it."

"What's he mean?" Dago asked.

"Get in the cab," Chopcock ordered.

"What's he mean?" Dago repeated after climbing into the back seat with Chopcock.

Instead of answering, Chopcock made an obscene motion, poking his index finger through a ring made by the thumb and middle finger of his other hand.

Dago was astonished. "Wow! How'd you know? They have shows like that in New York?"

"Not that I know of, but it figures."

The cab left the city and drove out into the countryside. The depth of the darkness matched that of being at sea at night. The stars appeared astonishingly large, and the songs of crickets made bucolic music. After ten minutes of rural roads, the cab stopped before what appeared to be a circus tent.

"Here we are, first nighters," the driver said. "It will cost you five bucks each if you want me to wait to take you back."

"You're a fucking bandit, you know that, Reb?" Chopcock growled belligerently.

"What the hell," Dago said, "We'll never find our way back without him."

"You owe me ten bucks between you," said the cab driver.

They had to pay the Negro ticket taker another five dollars apiece at the door flap to get in.

"I'm damn near broke," Chopcock complained.

"I got some money left," Dago reassured him. His loyalty to family and friends surpassed the understanding of most men. It was a way of life where he came from. Loyalty was the only commodity of value the residents could afford.

Inside, there were no seats. In the inadequate light cast by naked bulbs, a small knot of men, some servicemen from nearby army posts, some civilian war plant workers, stood silently staring at everything but each other. Presently, a hidden phonograph blared forth the pounding tones of "Stars and Stripes Forever" through the tobacco reeking air of the arena. The music halted as abruptly as it had begun and the audience became silent.

A tent flap parted at the far end of the encircling canvas and out stepped a stubble faced man with a curved beak of a nose and a chin that receded to near invisibility. A black ten-gallon hat was perched precariously on the back of his head and a red western shirt embroidered with black roses covered an imploded chest. His narrow pants, too, were black and his feet were shod in worn, tan alligator boots.

"Gentleman," the cowboy announced in a voice

husky with Lucky Strikes and Green River Whiskey, "we now present for your edification an act rarely seen since it was the star attraction in Rome's Coliseum. Your eyes will behold a gorgeous young woman enamored of a beast and a beast enamored of her. People will stare at you unbelievingly when you relate to them what you witnessed here today, but you will know, because you are here. And now, I present to you--ALICE AND HER ASS!"

Again the tent flap parted and from the gap, a naked Rubenesque woman emerged leading a donkey. Her skin was the color of ochre, her hips wide and her hair an unnatural blonde. Still, she was more attractive than Chopcock and Dago had expected.

The woman led the donkey to the center of the tent. The animal seemed to know the routine and followed docilely. The men's eyes were riveted to her. Perspiration beaded up on foreheads and tongues licked dry lips.

The woman placed her back against the center pole of the tent. Thick as a telephone pole, it made a perfect support for her body. She leaned back against the pole, still holding the donkey's reins. She smiled, bowed almost bashfully from the waist, her huge breasts flopping, and waved to her audience. As soon as her arm dropped she thrust out her pelvis and simultaneously released the donkey's reins. It was obvious that the beast had been through it before. The moment the woman's body arched out, the donkey's huge lingam slid from its sheath and dangled in the stale air, twitching and dripping. The flesh shaft in the dim light, the color of spoiled buttermilk, jerked spasmodically below the beast. Suddenly the donkey, with no coaxing from his human partner, leaped up and placed his forelegs on a cross pole above the woman's head as she, at the same time, guided his great member into her vagina.

"Jesus H. Tapdancin' Christ!" Dago exclaimed, while Chopcock gasped.

"He'll kill her with that thing," Dago said.

"Nah, she's used to it. They stretched her to his

size."

"Think so? The first time must have ripped her up, though."

"They probably broke her in with dildos. They probably started with a small one and put in larger and larger ones until she was ready for the big league."

Chopcock and Dago fastened their attention to the woman's face. Her eyes were bulging to a frightening extent as she thrust herself back and forth riding on the donkey's organ. Sweat coursed down her pumping body and it glistened in the yellow light. Her mouth was open in a silent scream as the donkey snorted, it's nostrils flaring, and its nates moving up and down.

"Think she likes it or is it just a job?" Dago whispered.

"Beats me."

Chopcock glanced at his wrist watch. "We better be getting back," he interrupted.

"What time is it?" asked Dago, his eyes still on the woman's contorted face.

"Eleven-thirty."

"Let's go," Dago said. "The skipper's a hard ass."

They walked out into the night air to the taxi. The driver, true to his word, was waiting for them.

"Great show, eh?" he drawled after they had sat down in the back seat.

Neither Chopcock nor Dago answered.

"I feel sorry for her," Chopcock told Dago.

"What a way to make a living," Dago said quietly, turned to the window, and peered into the darkness.

They drove in silence.

"Want a drink?" the cab driver finally offered, and picked up a pint bottle of whiskey lying next to him on the seat.

"Here, catch," the cab driver said without waiting for their reply.

Dago caught it, unscrewed the top, raised the bottle to his lips and took a long drink. He then pulled the bottle away from his mouth and coughed vigorously. He wiped his mouth with his sleeve and handed the bottle to Chopcock.

"I hate booze," Chopcock guped. "Got any tea? You know, grass."

"Huh?" the cabby said.

"Mary Jane, Schmuck. Marijuana."

"That's illegal."

"Yeah, you give a fuck," laughed Chopcock, and taking the bottle from Dago, drank. Then he, too, coughed a choking, throat-tearing cough.

Despite the unpleasant reaction they were having from the cheap whiskey, Chopcock and Dago passed the bottle between them until it was empty.

By the time the taxi came to a stop at the entrance to the small naval base, the two sailors were on the threshold of a drunk.

"I got something here I'm willing to bet you fellahs going to find right interesting," the driver promised.

"Yeah, like what?" questioned Dago.

"Now just hold on there and I'll give you a peek."

The cab driver reached down to the floor of the front passenger seat and came up with a straw basket. He lifted the lid like a chef uncovering his proudest dish. Inside, quietly cringing, was a small brown monkey.

"I'll sell him to you guys for ten bucks," proposed the cab driver.

"Who the hell needs a monkey, for Christ sake?" Dago said.

Chopcock stared at the animal and a smile appeared on his usually dour face.

"Wait a minute, Dago, I got an idea."

"Like what?"

"Suppose we buy the monkey."

"What?"

"Just suppose."

"Okay, I'm supposing," Dago said.

"And suppose we turn it loose on the ship?"

"Yeah?"

"And suppose when we're out to sea tomorrow

65

the crew suddenly sees this monkey swinging from the mast?"

Dago laughed.

"Won't that be something?" Chopcock asked.

"Let's do it."

"Give the guy ten bucks."

"Sure" Dago removed his wallet from the inside pocket of his dress blues and extracted his last ten dollar bill. He handed it to the driver and immediately demanded his property, "Give her here, Reb."

The cab driver thrust the basket into Dago's hands. The drunken sailors piled out of the cab and whistled their way past the Coast Guard sentry at the entrance.

"We did it," Chopcock said after they had left the sentry behind.

"He didn't notice a thing," Dago agreed.

"Probably thought it was something we bought in town. You know, Indian stuff."

They stopped in the dark just below the bow of the *1525*. They were pleased to observe that they could not be seen by the gangway officer from his post on the deck.

Chopcock opened the basket and put the monkey on the hawser leading up to the ship's bow. The monkey sat there bewildered at the behavior of his new masters.

"Boot his ass!" Dago cried.

Chopcock slapped the monkey's rump, and it had the desired effect. The animal fled up the bowline, but stopped at the metal rat guard barrier.

"He just sits there," Dago said in a voice turgid with disgust.

"Shoo!" Dago hissed. "Shoo! Climb over the thing you stupid son of a bitch."

"Hey, he listened to you," Chopcock said as he watched the monkey climb over the disk-shaped rat guard, scamper up the bowline to the deck, and disappear in the darkness.

"Dago, old buddy," Chopcock promised, "you and me are going to be legends in our own time."

***

The next morning the playing of "Oh, What a Beautiful Morning" was followed by the unfamiliar sound of laughter from crewmen gathered on the main deck staring up at the mast. On the yardarm, one hand holding the mast, the other hand moving the sheath of its scarlet penis up and down, was the monkey. The scene was almost out of control as one sailor after another collapsed on the deck laughing. A few of the men ran below decks to the crew's quarters to apprise the others of the astonishing sight. The crowd grew larger even as the laughter grew louder. Near pandemonium had erupted.

Attracted by the unusual sounds of merriment, Chief hurried to the place of its origin. What he saw made him gasp. He didn't know whether to order the men to disperse or to report it to a higher authority. After a second or two of thought, Chief decided dispersing the men would eradicate the symptoms but the source of the infection would remain. Chief raced for officer's country and headed for Brown's cabin. He found him staring into the mirror, razor in hand.

"Mr. Brown," Chief stumbled, not knowing quite how to begin to explain the strange event.

"Yeah, Chief, what is it?"

"There's something going on, sir,"

"Yeah, what?"

"Well, sir..."

"For Christ sake, Chief, spit it out."

"There's a monkey on the yardarm, sir," Chief reported almost apologetically.

"What?"

"A monkey on the yardarm, sir."

"A monkey? What the hell you talking about, Chief? You haven't been tapping the binnacle, have you?"

"No, sir."

"What the hell's a monkey doing up there, for

67

God's sake?"

"Right now he's whacking off, sir."

Brown's head swiveled from the mirror into which he had been staring and locked on Chief's eyes in which confoundment shone like beacons.

Brown dropped his razor and ran for the hatch leading to the deck.

"Come on, Chief, follow me!" he cried.

The men were now up on the conn shaking the mast, baiting the masturbating simian.

"What the hell's going on here?" Brown screamed.

"There's a monkey up there abeatin' his meat," answered a sailor.

Brown turned on his heels and ran back through the hatch, heading for the arms locker. He unlocked the cabinet, chose a .45 semi-automatic, and went back out on deck, waving the pistol like a cinema cowboy. Brown looked up at the mast. The monkey was gone.

"Where is he?" Brown screamed. "Where is he?"

None of the men answered.

Brown wheeled around and began to search for the monkey. He finally spotted him swinging through the guy wires. Brown raised his pistol and fired. The monkey, startled by the loud report, swung down onto the afterdeck. Brown pursued the primate waving his pistol. He finally chased it to the fantail. The monkey stopped and looked at Brown uncomprehendingly. Brown aimed the pistol at the monkey's head and pulled the trigger. The huge .45-caliber round blew the monkey's entire head off its neck. What was left of the monkey collapsed in a heap. Pieces of brain, skull, and blood flew in every direction. Brown approached the decapitated monkey smiling, lifted him up, waved him above his head triumphantly, and threw him overboard. Then he turned to face the horrified crewmen.

"Nice shootin', eh?" Brown bragged.

The sailors were silent. They stood in their places unable to move. They looked at Brown sullenly, then began to mutter obscenities.

"All right, men, disperse. I'm sure you've got work to do. Let's turn to."

The men stared defiantly at Brown.

"Move it!" Brown shouted.

They stood with obstinate eyes. The psychology of a lynch mob was in the air.

"Turn to or I'll put you all on report," Brown, warned, turned, and began to walk away.

"What's the color of shit?" came the voice of one of the sailors.

Brown spun on his heels and faced the rebellious sailors.

"Who said that?"

Not getting an answer from the angry men, he turned again to leave.

"What's the color of shit?" came another voice.

This time Brown did not turn to confront his antagonists. Instead, he fled through the hatch and back to his room screaming, "I'll court martial the bunch of you. Just wait and see."

***

The next morning, just after breakfast, the voice of Chief came thundering over the public address system.

"Now hear this. Now hear this. All hands who made liberty last night muster aft on the main deck in ten minutes."

Almost immediately, sailors appeared making for the designated assembling site. They fell into ranks with Chief at the head. Facing them was Lieutenant Brown and a man in undress blues with a Coast Guard emblem on his sleeve.

"Oh, oh," Chopcock whined.

"Shit!" Dago whimpered in anguish.

Chief faced a pallid Brown whose anger over the monkey incident was still a fresh wound. The insults had left an account that had to be settled. The men had revealed their disrespect for him and that was painful and diminishing.

"All present and accounted for," Chief reported after checking the men's names off on the liberty list.

"Okay, sailor," Brown said to the Coast Guardsman, "let's look them over."

"Aye aye, sir," the Coast Guardsman replied and smiled, seemingly happy to be the center of attention.

Together the Coast Guardsman and Brown walked the two ranks and peered into the face of each man in turn.

"Well?" Brown said after passing the last man.

"I can identify the two who were carrying a basket, sir."

"Point them out."

The Coast Guardsman walked back along the second rank, stopped in front of Dago, pointed to him and nodded to Brown. Brown smirked malevolently.

The Coast Guardsman stepped up to the next man, pointed to him and said, "This is the other one."

Brown showed his excitement by slapping his hands together.

"You're sure?"

"Yes, sir. No mistake possible."

Brown thundered, "You two, you two are on report."

"You've done a good job, sailor," he congratulated the Coast Guardman.

"Welcome, sir," replied the man and left with a jaunty step as Brown patted him on the back.

***

Captain Cadgett enjoyed sitting in judgment at a Captain's Mast or a Summary Court Martial. Having been an enlisted man himself, he knew every dodge, every excuse, every lie. He also knew that the punishments other skippers handed out were usually lenient: a few hours extra duty or deprived liberty. He was deliberately harsher. Being a mustang, Cadgett feared the men assumed they had his understanding and compassion. They did not, and they soon discovered it.

Standing before Cadgett were two men he believed were the most miserable creatures in his crew. Chopcock and Dago shifted from foot to foot nervously and twisted their white caps in their sweaty hands. Their faces betrayed their anxiety and Cadgett felt loathing for them well up in him. Chopcock's records showed Cadgett that the man had a high IQ. He would have been given a third class petty officer's rating when he graduated from signalman school, except for a series of minor lapses of discipline. Dago's records showed him to be slightly below average intelligence, not suited for a service school. A born deck ape.

Cadgett looked up from Chopcock's service record and shook his head disgustedly. "You're the one they call Chopcock?"

"Yes, sir."

"Why?"

"I'm circumcised, sir."

Cadgett suppressed a smile, then grunted. "And you're known as Dago?" he questioned shifting his gaze to the other man.

"Yes, sir."

"Don't they ever call you by your legal names?"

"The Chief does at muster, sir," explained Dago, while Chopcock nodded in agreement.

"Okay," Cadgett continued, "Where did you two get the monkey?"

"We didn't, sir," Chopcock responded. "You see, sir, we bought this basket, sir. It was an old Indian thing. We wanted to keep it as a souvenir of our visit to Florida, sir. Well, when we got near the ship we heard this noise coming from the basket. So we opened it to see what it was, and I'll be darned if a monkey doesn't jump out, run up the bowline, and jump aboard."

"And that's what happened? Say!"

Cadgett paused and looked at Dago. "That's what happened, Dago? Say!"

"Oh, yes, sir. We sure were surprised."

"Captain," Brown interrupted, "these are the same two who were arrested in New Orleans for refusing to move from the colored section of a street car."

"Oh, yes, I remember. Our two abolitionists."

"That was last time, Captain. This is for this time, sir."

"What are you, Chopcock, some kind of a sea lawyer?" Cadgett asked.

"No, sir, I'm just concerned about double jeopardy."

"Double jeopardy? Where did you learn about that?"

"The movies, sir."

Cadgett once more suppressed a smile. "The movies," he mumbled under his breath.

The captain stood up and thrust his face so close to theirs, they could smell his last cigarette.

"Now I'll tell you what I think. I think you two are trying to sell me a sea story, and your salesmanship isn't very effective. In fact, you men couldn't sell cunt in a lumber camp."

"We bought him from a cabby, sir," Chopcock confessed hastily.

"Why did you smuggle it aboard?"

"We were three sheets to the wind, sir," Dago said.

"Yes, sir," Chopcock added, "and when you're that way, things seem funny that aren't funny when you sober up."

"Good point," Cadgett admitted.

Chopcock and Dago smiled at each other.

"Okay," the captain said in an almost kindly voice, "Suppose we're under way and the monkey jumps on the helmsman. He loses control and we collide with another vessel."

Cadgett paused, awaiting a response. Getting none, his tone changed. "Well, say, goddamn you! Say!"

Chopcock and Dago stood silent.

Cadgett folded his arms in front of his chest and stared at the two miscreants for several long seconds. "Seventy two hours bread and water! Mr. Brown, have these two shitbirds locked up in the farthest compartment aft and station an armed coxswain at the door."

"Aye aye, sir," Brown said, parted the curtain and shouted, "Yeoman!"

Pens appeared almost immediately.

Chapter VII

After a one-day call at Key West, LST *1525* proceeded up the Atlantic coast en route to the Naval Ammunition Depot at Redbank, New Jersey. The voyage was uneventful except for a submarine alert off of Georgia and the usual rough seas near Cape Hatteras. Through all this, the crew performed acceptably and the ship showed no sign of malfunctions.

At Redbank, the crew lined the rail to watch large crates of ammunition being loaded onto the tank deck as cargo for the European Theater of Operations.

"I thought they had ammunition ships for this, for Christ's sake," a sailor remarked.

"If we get hit it's goodbye, Charlie," contributed another.

"There won't be enough of us left for the sharks to snack on," another said.

"I haven't done this since the last time I was in church, a long long time ago," Ensign Mullen said, and crossed himself.

Liam wandered up to the deck to watch the loading. He noticed Ensign Mullen at the rail and he took a place beside him. Together they watched the cranes hoist ammunition crates over the deck to the forward hatch and lower them onto the tank deck. There, the fork lifts took over. They stacked the crates starting aft, all the way to near the beginning of the tank deck. The amount of ammunition the *1525* carried was huge.

"Scary, isn't it?" Mullen commented to Liam.

"I'm not comforted by it," he answered.

"Where you from?" asked Mullen.

"San Francisco."

"Never been there," he admitted and patted down his wind-blown hair with his right hand.

"Great town for bachelors," Liam said without taking his eyes off the swinging crane.

Liam was impressed by Mullen. He liked the man's serious mien, his rare, shy smile, his thinning black hair, and especially his almost brutal features.

"Ever lift weights?" Liam asked.

"No," Mullen answered, still staring ahead.

"Remarkable," Liam observed, and without asking permission touched one of Mullen's biceps with his index finger.

"I'm to the muscles born," Mullen said. "How about you?" "I'll bet nobody on the beach kicks sand in *your* face."

"I've got to work at it."

Liam glanced up at the LCT that was secured to the deck in New Orleans. "Ugly looking things, LCTs. We're lucky we weren't assigned to one of them."

"Could have been," Mullen answered. "Half of everyone finishing training this year is being assigned to the amphibious forces. Nineteen-forty-four is going to be a big year for invasions."

"I saw an LCT in New Orleans," Liam said. "I never realized they were so big. They load any more on this ship the Germans won't have to torpedo us, we'll sink on our own." Without pause he added, "Where you from?"

"Cleveland."

"Nice place to live? For bachelors, I mean."

"It's okay," Mullen responded and added, "for bachelors."

Liam turned his attention back to the loading and marveled at the efficiency of the operating crews and their equipment.

"How long you been aboard?" Liam asked.

"I'm a plank owner."

"Fill me in on Cadgett."

"I don't know much more than you do". Mullen shifted his gaze off into the distance.

"Why do you think he reserves swearing to himself alone?"

Mullen turned slightly but didn't look at Liam directly. "Perhaps he thinks his cussing will have more impact that way."

"That makes sense," Liam added. "And what do you think about the .45?"

"Well, I've got to get going. Nice talking to you."

"Hey, not so fast," Liam said, grabbing Mullen's arm as he turned to leave.

"Let's make liberty together some time. You know, Liam and Pete, the Gold Dust twins."

"Sure," Mullen said, and looked searchingly into Liam's eyes.

***

Liam insisted that they not go uptown. That was where the enlisted men went on liberty—Central Park, Times Square, Columbus Circle. That was where the whores and the Victory girls were.

Liam recommended, too, that they avoid Queens where the bars were filled with lonely, middle-aged man-hunters.

Greenwich Village was the place Fitzpatrick suggested they visit.

They took the bus from Redbank to New York, where Liam offered to show him around, Mullen never having been to the city before.

Liam and Muller boarded a bus with an open top deck and rode it all the way down Fifth Avenue to Eighth Street. Snow was falling and their cheeks were wet and raw from the stinging cold. The men trudged through a deserted, gusty Washington Square Park to the San Remo where Mullen expressed surprise by the number of patrons crowded against one another. Most stood talking and sipping their beer, policed by the half dozen tough Sicilian cousins who worked in the hangout.

"It reminds me of San Francisco," Liam told Mullen.

"There's nothing much happening," Mullen said.

76

"They don't look as if they're having a good time."

"That's the whole idea," Liam told him. "They're detached. They don't even want to seem like they're having a good time. Good times are for the helots."

"Why, for Christ's sake?" Mullen exclaimed.

"It's—hep, I think the word is," Liam answered.

"There's a sickening smell of garlic, beer and urine here, for Christ's sake."

"Okay, let's strike out for greater opportunities of adventure," Liam offered cheerfully.

They walked into the icy night to Sixth Avenue. At the corner of Eighth Street, plows had piled the snow up along the avenue creating a long, dirty white berm. The two officers trudged through the snow barrier and stepped into the road. When they reached the other side, Mullen slipped on a thin layer of ice and Liam reached out to grab him. Each man's hand clasped the other. When the danger of falling was past and Mullen had righted himself, he did not let go and they continued, warm hand in warm hand.

***

As usual, Ritter walked the mile to the Bradford place on the old road leading there from his farm. The trip through the fields was shorter but it meant climbing over the crumbling stone wall that divided their properties, and possibly stepping in crusted cow pies concealed beneath patches of snow.

Once in the barn, Ritter hurried through the feeding chore he had voluntarily assigned himself. He didn't really mind. It put him a convenient position to visit the Bradford house.

After Ritter was done feeding Sierra he gave the animal a quick brushing. Sierra was a fine horse, he thought, not as beautiful or valuable as Ritter's two Arabians, but a superior animal by any standards.

Ritter had just about finished up when Nora appeared at the entrance to the barn.

"Nora! Didn't expect to see you. You're supposed to be at school."

She didn't trouble to greet him. She just began speaking to him impatiently.

"Dad's ship will be coming into Boston today. I'm driving up there to bring him home."

"That's nice," Ritter told her coolly.

"I don't want you to be here when we get back."

"And who's going to care for your nag?"

"I'll do it," she said.

Ritter turned away muttering. "That's the thanks I get," "I do it out of the goodness of my heart."

"The goodness of your hard on, is what you mean."

Ritter looked at her with contempt. She had a foul mouth. Always did, even as a twelve-year-old when he first saw her.

"Are those your orders or June's?" he asked with scorn in his voice.

"When you refer to my mother, you call her Mrs. Bradford."

"I'll sure do that," he responded smirking, "And when she's moaning "Walt, Walt", I'll tell her to call me Mr. Ritter."

Nora picked up a shovel that was leaning against the wall and drew it back to strike at him. Ritter leaped forward and grabbed her by the wrists, knocking the shovel to the ground. He felt his hands tighten and saw her wince.

Frightened by her show of pain, Ritter said, "I only grabbed you to protect myself. Don't go around saying that I attacked you."

"You bastard!" Nora cried and wrenched herself free from his now slackening grasp.

"There, I let you go," Ritter told her.

"Get out of here, you son of a bitch. Now!" Nora said.

CHAPTER VIII

The Coast Guardsmen would not permit Nora to drive her station wagon onto the dock in Quincy where the *1525* was tied up. She found a parking spot on a nearby street and walked to the guarded entrance, identified herself, and went up to the gangway. Seeing an attractive woman on the dock, the gangway officer hurried down to greet her.

"Can I help you, ma'am?" he said.

"Will you send word to Commodore Bradford that his daughter is here to pick him up?"

"Yes, ma'am. The Commodore told us to expect you. Come aboard. I'll send someone to tell him."

Nora followed him up the gangway to the deck.

"Oh, by the way, Mr..."

"Graves, ma'am."

"Could you tell me if Mr. Fitzpatrick is aboard?"

"Yes, he is, ma'am."

"Would you first tell Mr. Fitzpatrick that Nora Bradford is here and would like to see him?"

"I'll do that, ma'am," he said, and instructed his sailor assistant to deliver the message to Fitzpatrick.

"It's cold, isn't it, Miss Bradford?" Graves remarked.

"February in Boston, brrr," Nora answered.

"don't know whether I can ever get used to it," Graves told her. "I'm from southern Arizona."

"Indian country," Nora said smiling.

"Copper country now."

"Yes."

79

"Here comes Mr. Fitzpatrick," Graves said, when he saw the officer hurrying toward them from the forecastle.

"Nora," Liam called out long before he reached her, "how nice to see you."

Nora looked at him and her heart quickened.

Once at Nora's side he extended his hand in the offer of a handshake. She would not abide it. She bent toward him and kissed him, catching a whiff of his personal smell and the remnants of that morning's shaving cream, and that was delicious to her.

"Are you going to join us?" Nora asked. "You have two days."

"I put your family out enough at Christmas."

"We were happy to have you. Wouldn't have gotten roast turkey if you hadn't been there."

Liam laughed.

"My visit was a success after all."

"Oh, it was a success".

"I'm sorry, Nora, I've already made plans to spend these two days in Boston."

"Oh," Nora said, pausing to think. Then she asked, "Could we talk in private?"

"I don't know..."

"It's important."

"Come to my cabin."

Nora followed Liam into the forecastle and down the row of tiny curtained rooms to his cabin where he parted the curtain. Mullen was lying on Liam's bunk reading a Boston newspaper that had come aboard that morning with the mail. Seeing Nora just behind Liam, Mullen leaped to his feet.

"Excuse me," Mullen exclaimed.

"Nora Bradford, Pete Mullen."

"How do you do?" His surprised look turned inquisitive.

"Would you excuse us for a few minutes, Pete?" Liam requested.

Mullen stiffened. His brows wrinkled and his jaw tightened.

"Sure," Mullen said, scarcely hiding his annoyance.

After Mullen had gone, Liam invited Nora to be seated in the cabin's only chair. She sat, then removed a cigarette from a gold cigarette case and lighted it.

"Liam, I want you to come home with us." Nora paused as if deciding whether to say what she wished to. Finally her voice hardened with resolve. "People should ask for what they want or they may never get it, don't you think?"

Liam did not reply. Instead he looked at her questioningly.

"I want to continue our relationship", she said. "Nothing more than that. Only to stay in touch until the war is over." "I don't understand," Liam answered. "I said nothing to encourage a relationship, did I?"

"No."

"Then why?"

"Maybe it's just sexual, I don't know."

"I was hardly a good lover."

"I liked it."

What Nora had done with Liam was not a new experience for her. She had done it with a variety of men she found attractive. The gratification came from the uniqueness of the experience with Liam. Always her male partners had been in tumescence when she began. Liam had been flaccid when she took him. She had felt the sensation of his flesh going from soft to hard inside her, filling her mouth with his warmth. That experience gave her a sexual satisfaction she had never experienced before.

"I'm sorry, Nora, what you want is impossible."

"Would I be bore if I asked why?"

"It's best we leave it at that."

"All right," Nora said, getting to her feet. "There's someone else, isn't there?"

"Yes, There's someone else."

"I'm not giving up, Liam," she insisted, and left the room briskly.

Liam sank to the edge of his bunk.

When the curtains were pushed aside a minute later, Mullen was standing there. "What the fuck was that all about?" he demanded.

**

"I hope coming home doesn't set you back with your studies," Bradford commented to Nora as Mildred placed his dinner in front of him.

Nora waved her hand at her father as if to say, "Everything is under control."

"How do you like your chop, Charles?" June asked.

"Fine". He chewed the first piece. "How's Sierra?" Bradford asked.

"Wonderful," Nora answered. "I wish I had the time to do some riding."

"Ritter taking good care things, then?"

"As always," Nora said matter-of-factly as June looked away, an almost imperceptible touch of color in her cheeks.

"Nice of him to do that disagreeable job," Bradford commented. "You should invite him to dinner now and then. Entertain him. I'm sure you know ways to make him feel welcome. He deserves something for his pains. Don't you agree? Of course you do."

"He's out of town for a few days," June said.

"Oh?" said Bradford. "A pity. I'd like to see him again. After all, we do have a lot in common, horses and all."

Bradford, June and Nora finished dinner in silence, then went into the living room where they drank until they were drowsy, then went upstairs to their rooms.

As they undressed, Bradford asked June, "I suppose you're glad I didn't invite Fitzpatrick?"

"He doesn't belong here."

"You made that clear."

June smiled, "Let's have one for the road. You'll be away a long time."

"My very thoughts," he said, and rolled on top of her.

Afterward, he lay there thinking for a while.

"How's Nora doing in school?"

June got up and walked to the bureau, took a Chesterfield from a pack lying there and lighted it. She climbed back into bed, placed a pillow against the headboard and sat up, her back propped against it. She smoked silently.

"You missed my question".

"I'm sorry, Charles, what was it?"

"How's Nora doing in school?"

June waved the cigarette, making a wispy stroke of smoke in the air.

"I don't think she bothers to study much. It just seems to come naturally to her."

"What does she do with her time, then?"

"Are you being disingenuous?"

"What are you talking about?" Bradford asked and sat up.

Despite June's long practiced ability to seem steady when she'd been drinking, her words were slightly slurred.

"Your daughter, my dear Charles, is a whore."

"You're drunk," he snapped.

"That I am, but that hardly alters the facts."

"Goddamn you!" he swore. "You call Nora a whore? You're the whore!"

Bradford retreated to his side of the bed where he remained silent for several moments.

"I'm sorry," he said finally.

She didn't answer.

"I'm sorry," he repeated.

She stared at the ceiling.

"Don't you realize what your constant absences have done to us?" June cried.

Bradford suddenly pitied his wife. He hated to see her in anguish.

"Your daughter might have turned out differently if you had been around enough to be a real father and...." June failed to finish. Instead, she began to sob.

Bradford took June in his arms.

"I'm sorry". "But whether I was home or not I don't think would change the nature of who we are."

"It would have changed me."

"For the better, or worse?"

Now June dried her eyes on a corner of the pillowcase and smiled. It was a weak smile but enough to gratify Bradford, who kissed her nose, then her mouth.

"Let's not argue any more. This may be the last time we see each other. It's no secret that we're going to Europe. Otherwise we wouldn't be in Boston today and in Halifax by Saturday. Now let's get some sleep. I have to leave first thing in the morning."

"Good night," June whispered.

CHAPTER IX

In the wheelhouse, Captain Cadgett peered into the murk, trying to penetrate the blackness.

"It's darker than three feet up a bull's ass," he muttered.

As they neared Halifax, where they were to rendezvous with the rest of the ships that were to make up their convoy, it was far too cold to pilot the ship from the open navigation bridge. Bradford stood in the wheelhouse with Graves, who was Officer of the Deck. As usual, Liam stood by to fulfill any order from Bradford. It was Chopcock's watch. He was stationed near the annunciator while another man was on the wheel.

"A pity Lord Nelson is not here to enjoy your imagery, Captain," Bradford remarked dryly.

"Yeah," Cadgett said, and left the wheelhouse for his cabin through the chartroom door.

Bradford and Fitzpatrick remained behind. It was not long ago that these were dangerous waters and they wanted to stay alert until dawn. Hearing a sudden thump, Bradford turned to see Chopcock collapsed on the deck. Instinctively, Bradford and Liam rushed to his side and helped him to his feet. Bradford noticed the sweat on the boy's brow and his inflamed cheeks.

"What's wrong, lad?" Bradford asked concernedly after he and Liam propped Chopcock up against the bulkhead.

"I don't feel good, sir," Chopcock answered.

Bradford put his hand to Chopcock's forehead. "No wonder. You're burning up."

"I'm sick," he said.

"That you are," Bradford agreed. "Now you lay below right now and report to the pharmacist's mate."

"Aye aye, sir". Chopcock forced the words out. He was almost unable to speak.

Chopcock, with Liam's help, stumbled through the chartroom and down below to find Doc.

"He's a sick boy," Bradford muttered to Graves.

"They say he doesn't eat much," Graves related. "Doesn't like Navy chow. "If he's sick it's his own damned fault."

***

Captain Cadgett was furious. He slapped the bulkhead hard with his hand. "That son of a bitch!" he cried. "He and that candy-assed aide of his."

Cadgett left his room in a temper and stomped down the passageway to Bradford's cabin. Without announcing himself, he pulled open the door, startling Bradford, who with Liam, was looking over some recently decoded messages.

"Yes, Captain, what is it?"

"You relieved one of my men early this morning?"

"I did. The boy was feverish and unsteady on his feet. How is he? Did you get a report from the pharmacist's mate?"

Cadgett took a deep breath, trying to control his anger. He folded his arms on his chest and leaned forward from the waist. His eyes were ablaze.

"Commodore, the matter should have been reported to the Officer of the Deck. You should not have taken it upon yourself to relieve that man."

"You call him a man, Captain, but he is only a boy. It was he and that other boy you sentenced to medieval punishment. Bread and water!"

"I was within my rights to punish them according to regulations. You were not within your rights to relieve that sailor from his watch station."

"Do you want to reprimand me, Captain? If so, proceed."

"You will not tempt me into insubordination, sir," he growled, and whirled to face Liam.

"But as for you, Fitzpatrick, you've been hanging around my bridge like a fart in a phone booth and I'm sick of you. I don't want to see you on the bridge again unless you have business up there. Is that clear, Lieutenant?"

"Clear, Lieutenant," Liam answered.

"I am a lieutenant, but I am captain of this vessel and you will address me as such, Lieutenant."

Cadgett did not wait for Fitzpatrick's answer. Instead, he left, mumbling his irritation as he went.

"Quit while he was ahead," Liam pointed out bitterly.

Bradford just shook his head. He seemed to have become saddened, almost despondent.

"You should have come down hard on him, sir," Liam advised. "Dampened that fuse so that it never explodes."

"I don't know, Liam. I must be careful not to humiliate him. When I was a young ensign there was a skipper who was my mentor. I remember him saying once, 'Never forget, to the crew, the captain is a deity. Undermine his divinity and the ship will make a landfall in hell.' Hard as it is, I'll continue to try not to undermine his authority."

***

The convoy received word that they were being followed by a submarine the second day out of Halifax en route to Milford Haven in Wales. Cadgett ordered Chief to have the crew stand by for an announcement.

"Now hear this," Chief droned into the microphone, "Now hear this. Stand by for an announcement by the Captain." Immediately afterwards came the voice of Cadgett: "This is the Captain speaking. We have word that we're being followed by at least one enemy submarine. So wear your inflatable life belts at all times. Hear?"

The men took the news calmly. They had been through so many practice alerts over the past weeks that the announcement seemed like just another drill.

Bradford was the one who had related the news to Cadgett. He had gotten the information from a message decoded by Liam, whose main duty was acting as Bradford's communications officer. After handing the message to Cadgett, Bradford went below to his cabin where he and Liam awaited further word.

The next message was hand delivered by Sparks, the ship's leading radioman, and immediately decoded by Liam.

"Give it here," Bradford requested.

There was nothing in the message about the submarine. Carefully folding the paper, he slipped it into his pocket and went up to the wheelhouse. He found Cadgett calmly scanning a sea more purple than blue, with roiling swells and whitecaps that seemed to lick out in search of prey.

"Captain," Bradford said to his back.

"Yes?" Cadgett let his binoculars fall from his hands and turned in Bradford's direction.

"A message from the British corvette."

Cadgett reached out for the message. Bradford took it from his pocket and handed it over. Cadgett scanned it for an unusually long time to absorb so short a message. It was as if he were committing it to memory. Finally, he crumpled the paper in his hand and smiled. It was a smile that Bradford never liked. It always preceded some sort of order that caused unnecessary discomfort for one or all of the crew.

"Flags!" Cadgett shouted, calling the signalman. t "Send the following message by blinker to that corvette yonder:' Your message warns that if we show a light at night you will shoot it out with machine gun fire. This is my reply: Just so much as point a machine gun in our direction and we'll rake your stem to stern with 40mm cannon fire. Signed: V.J. Cadgett, Commanding, United States Ship LST *1525*."

"You were unnecessarily belligerent, Captain," Bradford said, when the signalman was out of earshot.

"Reckon I was," Cadgett answered, "but so were they."

"I would prefer you be more diplomatic, Captain".

Brown, who had over heard the conversation, asked, "You think there really is a U-boat following us, Commodore?"

Bradford looked at Brown as if he had never seen him before. "Yes, and you can bet there's a pack of them ahead waiting for him to radio them our heading."

"Then tonight they'll be all over us like flies on shit," Cadgett observed.

"Well said," Bradford answered, not bothering to hide the distaste in his voice.

"The tank deck's jammed with one hundred and thirty-five box cars of ammunition," Cadgett smiled. "Are you worried, Commodore"?

"I am, and you should be too."

Brown interrupted, "Maybe they'll set their torpedoes depths too low. We have the shallowest draft of any ship our size. That's happened before and..."

"Torpedoes have passed under LSTs, but that was weeks ago," Cadgett dismissed the argument. "The Germans learn fast."

"Just thinking, Captain." Brown added. "Since we may be in action tonight, why not have the cook rustle up some traditional pre-battle steak and eggs?"

"It's a little outdated, Mr. Brown, but why not?". "Better to die on a full stomach, eh, Commodore?"

Instead of replying, Bradford left the wheelhouse looking troubled.

"Mr. Brown, lay below and tell the cook we want a traditional pre-combat dinner tonight," Cadgett said.

"Aye aye, sir". Brown hurried to give the instruction as if it were his own.

***

Since the LST *1525* was not designed to be a

flagship, there was no extra room for a flag officer and his staff. At mess, the officers were jammed in as tightly as the enlisted men at their meals.

There was an air of festivity at that evening's meal. The excitement of the possibility of action that night or early the next morning, in addition to the anticipated steak and eggs, had the young officers in a happy mood.

"Move over, fat boy," Graves jested as he squeezed into his place next to Williams.

"Up yours with a dogging bar," Williams returned, chancing that Cadgett would not object to the figure of speech.

He was right. Considering the possible events to follow, Cadgett was prepared to tolerate a reasonable amount of adolescent antics.

"Anything happen on your watch?" Butterly asked Cornell.

"No. It was quiet as a mouse urinating on cotton," Cornell answered, employing a euphemism in a fanciful allegory he had once heard Cadgett use.

Cadgett did not join in the revelry, but neither did he intervene. He remained silent, unsmiling but uncomplaining about the bravado.

"This is what we've been waiting for, a chance to fight," Graves boasted.

"You're forgetting we don't go after them, they go after us," Butterly said.

"I can swim," Cornell replied with a dismissive chuckle.

"You guys think you're tough," Brown snarled. "You won't feel like joking if the ammunition loaded on our tank deck blows."

It grew quiet, the young officers appearing to conjure with Brown's words.

"Even if you survive the explosion, which is unlikely," Brown went on, "you'll be dead a few minutes after you hit the water. That's how cold the ocean is."

"Hey, here comes the feast!" Butterly shouted as the stewards entered carrying plates of steak and eggs.

"Let me at it," Cornell cried grabbing his fork and knife.

"Look at the size of those steaks!" Williams exclaimed as he watched the stewards distribute them.

"I'd love to see the faces of the crew when they get this instead of creamed beef on toast," Graves chuckled.

"Darned if I didn't forget to include the crew," Brown said.

Bradford paused, laid his fork down, then pushed his plate away.

"What's the matter, Commodore? The steak not cooked to your taste?" Cadgett asked between chews.

Bradford stared straight ahead, unresponding. Then Liam pushed his plate away. The officers watched as the drama unfolded, then they, too, stopped eating.

"What the hell's going on here?" Cadgett demanded.

Nobody replied. Instead, they lowered their eyes.

Cadgett stared at his officers in a frigid fury.

One by one, they slowly began to eat again, chewing the formerly coveted meal with obvious distaste. Cadgett and Brown resumed eating, their eyes on the officers all the while.

Bradford and Liam rose from the table and left the wardroom.

Cadgett, and the other officers glumly continued their meal. Brown was satisfied. He had repaid the crew for humiliating him.

* * *

The wolf pack did not attack that night or the entire next week. It happened one freezing morning between Iceland and the Azores. Not the more survivable cold experienced on land, but a wet cold no clothing could completely keep from penetrating, Navy foul weather gear included. The lacerating winds swept over the agitated surface of the sea, absorbing an invasive moisture against which there was no real defense. The frigid wind froze the eyelids shut and stiffened exposed skin until it was dead numb.

From the wheelhouse, the Officer of the Deck, Ensign Williams, watched the men of the bow watch who had been relieved stumble aft through the lashing wind to the superstructure.

"Eerie the way the krill in the spindrift make the men glow," Williams commented as the luminescent, wraith-like figures came toward them.

Williams was a smiling, smooth faced young man with friendly blue eyes, untrainable brown hair, and a likable teen-aged insouciance.

"Like ghosts, ain't they?" the sailor on the annunciator agreed.

"It's beautiful, really beautiful," a near-recovered Chopcock, who was on the helm, said almost inaudibly.

"Gives me the creeps," Williams said, ignoring Chopcock's quiet remark.

The vessel ran silently, plowing into the frigid night along with its forty-eight companion ships in the convoy.

A sudden faint flicker of orange flashed from a Norwegian freighter on their port side. The light began to grow and soon it was an unmistakable flame.

"Mr. Williams," Rafferty, the sailor on the annunciator, called out, "I think the ship to port is afire."

Williams turned, glanced through the porthole and saw flames jump into the air and spread across the freighter's deck.

"Oh, my God!" Williams cried, his eyes darted around the wheelhouse. He ran to the bulkhead and grabbed the phone to the captain's cabin. Then he froze. "The captain doesn't have that cabin anymore," he said. "Coxswain, go get the captain!"

The coxswain, a skinny, nervous little man ran frantically around in circles.

Chopcock, seeing the coxswain's confusion, turned to Ensign Williams, "I'll get the captain, sir."

Flags hesitated, then stepped forward to take the helm.

"No, wait, Chopcock," Williams countered.

92

"We'll need someone on the super conn who can read blinker. Get up there, now!"

Williams grabbed the coxswain by the shoulders and shook him.

"Now you listen to me, sailor. Pull yourself together and go down and get the captain or I swear I'll deck you right now." With that, Williams balled his fist, pulled his arm back and was ready to let go when the coxswain seemed to miraculously recover.

"Aye aye, sir," he whimpered and fled through the chartroom to Cadgett's cabin.

Chopcock, faced with the ladder to the platform held up by what seemed flimsy stanchions, took a deep breath and carefully began to climb. He took one frozen rung at a time, feeling it first to make sure his ungloved hand would not slip, then pulled himself up, fastening his shoes one at a time to the slippery rung below. He cursed himself for not wearing gloves, but with his watch station in the wheelhouse, he never expected to be out in the open for long. After he climbed each rung, he rested while looking at the flaming freighter to port. Men were jumping into the freezing sea rather than burn to death aboard the torpedoed ship; He knew they would not last long in water. He could see that the British escort vessels were more interested in dropping depth charges than in rescuing the men floundering in the sea.

Chopcock climbed another rung with a hand so numb that he could not feel it touch the metal. He stopped again to watch the escorts charging between the lanes of ships, dropping depth charges.

At long last, Chopcock made it to the top of the ladder and hoisted himself onto the super conn where he crouched behind the thin plywood apron surrounding the platform, trying to get some protection from the blasting wind. He peered into the dark and waited. From the super conn it looked like a hundred-mile drop to the deck. If the ship were hit by a torpedo, Chopcock he knew would stand the least chance of anyone aboard of surviving.

Far off the port bow, there was a sudden, stunning yellow flash, as if the sun exploded. As the great light faded into darkness, Chopcock could see the convoy laid out below him, the escorts dashing between the columns of ships like frenzied beagles after fleeing foxes, and behind, the freighter sinking.

Chopcock knew the flash meant another ship had been torpedoed, probably one carrying a volatile cargo, to cause so brilliant a light. It heightened his anxiety and he was even more frightened than before.

Chopcock began to flail his arms in a vain attempt to warm himself while wondering why he had heard no explosion when the ships were torpedoed. Had his mind blocked the noise?

Somewhere, far off the port bow, a light suddenly glared. It shone for one eerie moment, an ephemeral specter, then disappeared, the blackness reclaiming the night in an instant. The unexpected signal startled Chopcock into wide eyed alert. The flash was a *daw*, blinker code for "Do you read me?" The required answer was *dot-daw-dot*: "Go ahead with your message."

Absorbing the portent of the signal, Chopcock panicked. Turning on his own blinker light to acknowledge the signal would reveal his ship's position to other U-boats in the wolfpack which were sure to be maneuvering in the darkness for firing positions.

Chopcock felt his sweat begin to run despite the freezing cold. Should he put the remaining ships and their hundreds of crewmen at risk? Perhaps whoever was out there had an important life or death message for the *1525*. Then again, it could be a U-boat ruse to sucker some dumb signalman into giving away the convoy's position.

The agony of choice was not Chopcock's only emotion. He reacted with self-righteous anger at the Navy for making him responsible for the safety of all those other ships and men. He was only a signalman striker, neither trained nor paid to make such awful decisions. He had just turned eighteen a couple of months before and had been in the Navy barely six months. He thought he could feel the sweat on his body begin to congeal from the frigid air. His skin crawled with itching as if his body were teeming with insects. His mind tumbled in confusion. Chopcock began to shout protestations into the blackness: "Goddamn it! Goddamn it to hell!"

Almost unconsciously, in response to his training, Chopcock painfully extended his arm to rest his hand on the blinker light's lever. His fingers were so numb, he could not feel whether or not they actually rested on the steel handle. He had to rely on his blurred, sleet-clogged eyes to judge their position. With no forethought, he jerked his hand down on the lever. The blinker's shutters clattered open and a shaft of white light shot over the surface of the sea to an unseen horizon. Shocked by what he had done, he immediately released the lever. He had signaled a *dot*.

"Well, that does it," Chopcock remonstrated with himself aloud. "I wrote my own death warrant, I might as well sign it." He pressed down on the lever, waiting a couple of beats before releasing it. He had signaled a *daw*. Now he purposefully flashed a *dot*, the final short flash of light telling every ship for miles around that he had received a signal and was inviting a reply.

Chopcock now tried to remove his hand from the lever, but the frozen sweat on his bare fingers had fastened them to the steel of the handle. Frantic, like an animal with a paw caught in a trap, he tore his hand away. He instinctively knew that he had left skin stuck to the handle.

Chopcock stared into the darkness, awaiting the message for which he had put so much at risk. He put his hands inside the pockets of his foul-weather jacket. He waited. His hands warmed a bit and the more they warmed, the more they pained. Ten minutes. Nothing. No explosions of torpedoed ships. No movement but the pitch and yaw of his clumsy, flat bottomed ship; no further signal from the origin of the mysterious light.

Chopcock dropped to his knees to take advantage of the pitiful protection afforded by the plywood ap apron around the platform. He folded his hands and rested them on the top rail of the apron. He could not stop his teeth from chattering and he blinked furiously to keep the sleet on his eyelashes from blinding him. His bladder opened from tension, and he actually welcomed the warmth of the urine as it coursed down his leg. He would not relax until daylight when, he had been told, U-boats seldom attack escorted ships.

Somehow the word had spread that there was trouble. Bradford and Fitzpatrick came charging up to the wheelhouse tucking their shirts into their trousers. Brown arrived in his underwear, wide-eyed and sweating. Cadgett and the coxswain messenger were already present, having been the first to arrive.

"Why the hell didn't you sound general quarters, Williams? Say! Say!" Cadgett demanded in a fury.

"I, I, was waiting for you, sir," Williams stammered.

"Well, sound it now, hear?"

"Aye aye, sir," said Williams and pulled the alarm lever.

Chief arrived last. But no sooner had Williams sounded the alarm than Chief had the microphone in his hand.

"Now hear this. Now hear this. General Quarters. General Quarters. All hands man your battle stations. This is not a drill. This is not a drill."

At the words "this is not a drill," the men leaped from their bunks and hurried to their stations, grabbing their steel helmets and life belts as they moved.

The crew stood at their battle stations in the arctic cold for nearly two hours. Many, in their haste, had not put on their foul weather trousers, and the cold began to tell. They suffered through the numbing agony, silently waiting for whatever it was out there that interrupted their sleep; they watched as the burning freighter behind them began to sink. Soon, with a great shudder, the ship dove into the sea and was gone.

***

Deciding there were no further attacks forthcoming, Cadgett took inventory of how his crew performed during its first genuine general quarters. Except for Williams's timidity, he was satisfied. He looked around. Bradford was alert and concerned. He peered out to the sea with intense concentration. Fitzpatrick was relaxed, his back up against the bulkhead, standing by, waiting for Sparks to deliver messages for him to decode for Bradford. Brown stood in his underwear peeking out of the port as if afraid to expose himself fully. He seemed almost paralyzed. His eyes were staring, his lower lip protruding and his forehead was wet. His hands trembled slightly, and he clasped them together to make it appear less obvious.

Cadgett growled at him, "Why in hell didn't you put on a pair of britches before showing up here? Goddamn you, don't you ever walk around this ship again with your pecker hanging out, hear?"

Brown tried to answer Cadgett but nothing escaped his mouth but a throaty gurgle.

"Looks like it's over," Cadgett said, returning to business. "Chief, have the crew secure from general quarters."

Cadgett spun around, heading for the chartroom door. "Brown, come with me!"

Brown, his hand covering his crotch, sheepishly followed Cadgett into the chartroom. Cadgett closed the door and positioned his face inches from Brown's. "Next time, stay below. I can't have the crew seeing my executive officer looking nervous as a whore in church. Hear?"

"Hear?" Cadgett repeated. "Say! Goddamn you, say!"

"Aye aye, sir," Brown finally managed to utter.

***

Graves didn't go back to sleep when the order to secure from battle stations was announced. Instead,

he went to the wardroom and drank a cup of coffee.
He then reported to the wheelhouse.

"You're relieved, Williams," Graves said to him.

"The only way I'll be relieved is when I see the
coast of England out there."

"You and me both, buddy," Graves concurred,
and took the binoculars from Williams.

Williams, a look of relief on his face, started for
the chartroom door to go below. He was stopped by
Chief. "Chopcock's still up on the super conn, Mr.
Williams," he told him.

"Oh, Christ, I forgot all about him. Call him
down, Chief."

Chief left the wheelhouse and climbed the ladder
to the navigation bridge. He grasped one of the temporary steel stanchions supporting the super conn's
platform. He held on tightly to keep from being
blown across the bridge by the blasts of freezing
winds that swept in without respite.

Cupping his hands around his mouth Chief
shouted up to the super conn. "Chopcock! Hey,
Chopcock! You're relieved." There was no response.
He shouted again, "Chopcock. Secure from your
watch. You're relieved, dammit. Get your ass down
here!"

Williams hurried to Chief's side. "Well? Where
the hell is he?"

"Don't know, sir. I've been yelling like a ban-
shee. He doesn't seem to hear."

"Here, let me try," Williams said, and shouldered
the Chief aside. He grabbed the stanchion with both
hands and shouted up into the wind.

"Chopcock, come on down. Chopcock, you're
relieved. Come on down, Chopcock. We haven't got
all day."

There was no reply.

"You're going to have to go up there, Chief. Tell
him he's on report for sleeping on watch."

"Aye aye, sir". Chief reluctantly approached the
ladder.

After a painful climb, Chief hoisted himself onto
the super conn. He found Chopcock curled up in the

fetal position in a corner of the platform.

"You no good son of a bitch," Chief shouted at him. "Wake up and get you ass down on the deck!"

He crawled to Chopcock, grabbed him by the shoulders, and shook him violently. "You're on report, shitbird. You'll be on bread and water for a week for this. Now wake up!"

Chopcock did not move. Instead, his head dropped to his shoulder and the upper part of his body fell forward onto Chief's chest.

Chief grabbed Chopcock by the shoulders and laid him out on the platform. He looked down at his face, first puzzled, then shocked. Chopcock's face was blue-white. There were patches of ice on his cheeks and his eyes were frozen half open as if he had tried to keep from falling into a last and final sleep.

Chief slapped Chopcock's face. First gently, then more vigorously. There was no response. He felt the boy's pulse. There wasn't a flutter.

Chief crawled to the edge of the platform on his knees and shouted down to Williams. "Can't wake him, Mr. Williams."

"Kick him," Williams replied.

"Won't do any good, sir."

"What the hell you talking about?"

"Something's wrong, sir."

"The hell you say! Kick him hard. The cold put him to sleep."

"He's asleep, all right, sir, but permanently."

"What? What do you mean, permanently?"

"He's dead, sir."

"You're crazy. Feel his pulse."

"Did, sir. Frozen stiff. Deader than Dewey's nuts, sir."

"Oh, my God," Williams cried. "I left him up there too long. Get the captain! Call the captain!" With that, he sank to the deck, put his head in his hands and wept.

***

They carried Chopcock's body below decks and laid him on the crew's mess table. Doc, the pharmacist mate, went through the prescribed steps to make certain he was dead, but he had no need to. The boy was a frozen hunk of flesh, more like a shrunken slab of meat than something that had been a human being.

Cadgett was there, seemingly unmoved by Chopcock's death.

"Yeah, he's gone," the pharmacist mate announced matter-of- factly.

"It was my fault, Captain," Williams sputtered through his tears.

"Shut up, Williams!" Cadgett said. "Stop your whining!"

"He'd be alive, Captain, if I paid attention to what I was doing."

"Bat shit!" Cadgett growled. "He didn't die because you forgot him up there; he died from dumb. Old fashioned dumb."

Cadgett bent down and pulled up Chopcock's shirt revealing his cotton skivvy undershirt. "No long johns."

Cadgett dropped the shirt and picked up Chopcock's lifeless hand.

"Not even gloves. This kid died the first chance he got," Cadgett said with contempt. "Doc, dispose of the body tonight. Make sure nobody's around."

"Aye aye, sir". The pharmacist's mate said, showed no surprise at Cadgett's order.

"As for you, Williams, stop acting like you squat to piss. You'll see a lot more dead before we head home. You'll probably be one of them yourself. Now get your ass out of here."

After Cadgett and Williams had left, the pharmacist's striker pulled Chopcock's skivvy shirt up to his chest revealing a partially healed scabby rash running from his hip to the full extent of one buttock.

"Hey, Doc, look here," the striker called to the pharmacist's mate.

Doc inspected the lesions with a practiced eye.

"Herpes Zoster," he pronounced.

"That what killed him?"

"No."

"Venereal?"

"No, it's from being rundown. Lack of sleep. Anxiety. That kind of thing."

The striker listened to the more experienced man with close attention. "Herpes Zoster, eh?" he said.

"They call it shingles," said Doc.

"How long's he had it?"

"Weeks maybe. Some of it has healed."

"He should have said something back in Boston. He'd be in the hospital now, stateside."

"Maybe the kid was tougher than the captain thought. It's an excruciatingly painful condition, yet he never complained about it."

"Well, let's get the body below," the striker sighed.

"Yeah," Doc agreed.

***

The next day Cadgett and Bradford came upon each other in the passageway. "I'm sorry about that boy, Captain," Bradford told him.

"Don't waste your time grieving".

Bradford looked at Cadgett with a mixture of puzzlement and shock.

"What time is the ceremony?" he asked, resisting the temptation to reply to Cadgett's remark.

"We're not having one."

"Not having one? Why?"

"For the safety of this ship," Cadgett replied.

"What has that to do with giving that boy a decent burial at sea?"

"I'll tell you what it has to do with it. The crew's been on watch four-hours-on, four-hours-off. They're tuckered out. They need every minute we can spare to rest. Their efficiency has been impaired by lack of sleep. The ship comes first. We don't have the luxury of wasting time on a ceremony for a kid who don't deserve it nohow."

"What in God's name are you saying, Cadgett?

101

He died while in action."

"He died, Commodore, because he was too vain to wear long woolen underwear."

"Captain, we must bury that boy with honor."

"Do you have the authority to order it, sir? This is, after all, my ship.

I'm willing to let a higher authority decide if you wish, Captain."

Cadgett began to laugh.

"I'd rather not test that, Commodore. But you wouldn't want me to be right one of these times."

"Will you or will you not carry out a burial-at-sea?"

"All right. I'll have the pharmacist's mate confine him to the sea, and I'll provide two side boys. That's all I can spare."

***

At sundown, it was sleeting. The sky could not be seen, and the arrival of night merely laid an additional layer of darkness on the black waters of the North Atlantic.

The pharmacist's mate and his striker carried the canvas in which Chopcock was sewn to the fantail of the ship. There, two sailors in dress blues and Liam and Bradford waited. There was no chaplain to read over the man. The pharmacists each grabbed a side of the canvas coffin and slipped it under the ship's railing into the sea while Liam, Bradford, and the sailors stood by saluting. Dago watched from the 40mm gun tub above. They did not see the bag hit the water, nor did they hear any splash. They just waited a few moments until they were sure he had sunk beneath the surface and then silently dispersed. Dago stayed for several minutes after they left, his teary eyes fastened to the spot where he had last seen Chopcock's body. Then he too, left.

***

The convoy arrived in the safety of British waters

only two ships shy of the forty-nine it began with. In Milford Haven, the *1525* unloaded its cargo of munitions and the LCT on its forward deck. The view from the bridge was no longer obstructed and the temporary super conn on which Chopcock froze to death was dismantled.

The first order to the crew upon anchoring was to air bedding topside. The smell in the crew's quarters had become fetid during the long trans-Atlantic voyage.

All heard the announcement over the PA system except Dago, who had been experiencing terrifying nightmares since Chopcock's death. He feared the dreams so much that he forced himself to stay awake. He finally passed out from exhaustion, sleeping as if he had joined his friend in death.

Brown, with the coxswain at his heels, inspected the crew's quarters to make certain the all-hands evolution had been obeyed. To the coxswain's surprise, Brown did not appear to be angry at finding Dago in his near comatose state. Instead, Brown looked down at the sleeping figure with feigned compassion.

"I'll wake him, sir," the coxswain said, and he stepped forward to shake Dago into consciousness.

"Let the poor boy sleep," Brown said, with a small smile. "He needs his beauty rest."

The coxswain, a puzzled look on his face inspired by Brown's seeming concern for a crewman, stepped back.

Brown dismissed the coxswain and hurried to see the captain. He stood outside his cabin and whispered through the closed curtains, "Captain, are you in, sir?"

"What?" Cadgett responded.

"It's me, sir, Brown."

"Just a moment," said Cadgett, then, "Okay, come in."

Brown parted the curtains and entered the tiny compartment. Cadgett was seated at his desk, upon which the photograph Brown had never seen lay face down.

"We've had an incident, sir."

"What's it this time, Brown, a gorilla poguing Fitzpatrick 'tween decks?"

"It's that goof-off they call Dago. I checked the crew's quarters to see that everyone aired bedding and sure enough he was sound asleep."

"Don't say?"

"He's contemptuous of you, sir. He needs to be taught a lesson."

Cadgett nodded his head, thinking. After what seemed to Brown an interminably long time, he looked up at his executive officer. "Okay, let's get him up here."

Brown moved to the curtain and shouted, "Pens!"

"Yes, sir," Pens replied, almost immediately.

"Get me Dago's service record, then get him up here."

"Aye aye, sir".

Pens woke Dago. He shook him hard, but Dago was as near to death as a man could get with a still-beating heart.

"Hey, Dago, wake up!" Doc yelled. "Get your ass out of that sack."

Dago stirred, but continued to sleep.

Pens grabbed Dago's arm and pulled him from the bunk, sending the young sailor tumbling to the deck.

"For Christ's sake!" Dago said rubbing his eyes unstuck and chomping his jaws to bring a little moisture to his mouth. "Why did you do that?"

"Lay up to the captain's room. He wants to see you. And right now."

"Oh, okay," Dago said, painfully sat up, stretched, then got to his wobbly knees.

"Follow me," Pens ordered.

Entering the captain's room, Dago was puzzled to see Brown standing just behind and off to the side of Cadgett.

"You're charged with disobeying orders," Cadgett announced.

"That's bullshit," Dago almost said but caught himself and changed it to a meek, "What?"

Brown said, "That's right. You disobeyed a direct order, an all-hands evolution to air bedding. You were asleep. The captain's orders apply to everyone but you, don't they, Dago?"

"All right, Mr. Brown," Cadgett cautioned.

Dago's eyes moved from Cadgett's impassive face to Brown's, which had taken on the look of a man who had just caught the big one. Dago licked his lips and shifted from one foot to the other.

Cadgett spoke again. "Dago, why didn't you get your bedding topside? Say, Dago, say!"

"Honest, Captain, I didn't hear the order. I've been tired, Captain, I haven't been sleeping."

"Yeah, well, we're all tired, Dago," Brown said.

"Usually Dillman wakes me if I have to get up," Dago continued. "This time he didn't. I think he was on watch himself."

Brown sneered and put his hands on his hips. "Don't hand us that. It's not the first time you caused trouble."

"I know that, Mr. Brown, but I swear I didn't hear the order. I slept right through it."

Cadgett said nothing for a few moments while Brown intently watched his face.

"Mr. Brown, leave us for a while," Cadgett said.

Brown hesitated, then walked out of the room casting a concerned look over his shoulder.

Cadgett waited until he was sure Brown was out of earshot. His face was hard, unyielding. He looked at Dago with no compassion. "I believe you, Dago. But there's nothing I can do. I can't risk undermining ship's discipline by going against my executive officer. I'm going to have to find you guilty. You're busted down to Second Class Seaman."

Dago reacted with a look of outrage, his words, though, were a relatively mild protest. "It's not fair, Captain. It's not fair."

"You won't understand this, Dago, but it is fair. Next time it could be someone else, the yeoman, Mr. Brown, yes, even me. You're dismissed."

Dago staggered from the Captain's cabin shaking

his head in disbelief.

"Pens!" Cadgett called, "Ask Mr. Brown to come back in."

"Aye aye, sir," Pens answered and scurried to find Brown.

He did not have to search far. Brown was waiting anxiously at the end of the passageway. He followed Pens back to the captain's cabin and entered with caution, as if afraid of what he was going to find.

"Brown," Cadgett told his executive officer, "you know that order we got to supply a man for that small boat group they're forming in Cornwall? Dago's your man."

"Thank you, Captain," Brown said, relieved.

"Thanks for what, Brown?"

"I'll cut the orders immediately, Captain," Pens said.

"Do that, Pens, and get him off the ship fast. I don't ever want to have to look him in the face again."

"Aye aye, sir," Pens said.

***

Brown was afraid things were turning against him over the Dago affair, but in the end he got out of it, he believed, with barely a scratch. That was only as it should be, he reasoned. After all, he had only been doing his duty.

Cadgett was difficult for Brown to figure. Hard as Brown tried to please him, Cadgett seemed doubtful about Brown's dedication. At any rate, he was rid of that goof-off Dago and he hoped Cadgett appreciated his help.

Back in his room Brown started to lie down in his bunk when he realized sweat was trickling down his body. It meandered down his torso in tiny rivulets and from his forehead it came in streams. He undressed, took a long, tepid shower, then picked up *Esquire*, and lay down in the bunk. He flipped the pages of the magazine looking at the drawings of the semi-nude, freakishly long-legged women.

106

Lost in the arousing pictures, Brown was suddenly aware of his name being called. "Mr. Brown, it's me, Pens. May I come in?"

"Sure."

Pens came into the room and stood by his bunk with a sheet of paper in his hand.

"Yeah, what is it, Pens?'

"The Captain wanted me to give you this, sir."

"Christ, you'd think it could wait till morning. Can't he run this ship without me for five minutes?"

Brown refused to take the document out of Pen's hand. "Well, don't just stand there, tell me what it's about."

"It's your transfer, sir."

"Transfer? What the hell are you talking about? *I* haven't requested a transfer."

"I have it right here in my hand, sir."

Still not deigning to read the paper, Brown objected, "It must be for that motor mac in the black gang. But he spells his name *B-R-O-W-N-E*. Come on, Pens, get yourself squared away."

"No, sir," Pens answered innocently. "It's for you, sir." The skipper distinctly said, 'Give this to Lieutenant Brown.'"

"Let me see that!" Brown insisted, then leaped out of his bunk and grabbed the paper from Pen's hand. The more he read the more agitated he became.

"Take it easy, sir," Pens cautioned.

"Get out of my way!" Brown cried, and roughly pushed the yeoman from his path. He raced down the passageway waving the paper in his hand.

"Captain! Captain!" Brown shouted.

When he reached the captain's cabin he tore open the curtain and confronted Cadgett. "This is a mistake, isn't it? It's got to be a mistake."

Cadgett looked up at his uninvited visitor, then reached for the photograph and turned it over. "It's no mistake. It's for you, Brown."

"But, Captain, why? I wouldn't let those punk young officers say bad things about you behind your back. I was loyal, Captain. Why are you doing this?"

"I'll tell you why, Brown. You've disgruntled the crew one time too many. They'll take a lot from their captain. From anyone else, it begins to affect their morale and then their efficiency. This ship must be an efficient ship, Brown. That's why you have to go."

"But, Captain...."

"I want you off this ship today!"

***

Mail was delivered aboard the LST *1525* just before the ship received orders to weigh anchor and proceed around Land's End and through the English Channel to Plymouth.

There was a letter to Liam from Nora. He nearly threw it away unread, but at the last moment, he changed his mind.

> Dear Liam:
>
> I am back at school now catching up on the work I missed during the time I took off to see Dad (and you, dammit!) in Mass.
>
> I must tell you that I can't stop thinking about you. (What Sierra must have thought!)
>
> I believe you when you say there is another, but I am patient. You and your "someone else" will be separated a long time during this war and who knows if she'll be there for you when you come home.
>
> Please look after Dad for

us. Sometimes I think he is
much too kind and sensitive to
be a tough naval commander,
hanging mutineers from the
highest yardarm and that sort
of thing.

Mother sends her best.
Please write.

Love,
Nora

Liam was disturbed by her letter. A rush of con-
flicting emotions overwhelmed him. He sank into a
chair and tried to deal with it. Why had he responded
to her in the stall? He never thought it possible and
yet there it was. Before he could do anything else,
even read the letter from his father, he grabbed paper
and pen and wrote a reply to Nora's letter.

Dear Nora,

Your letter obviously came by airmail,
as it was waiting for me when we
arrived overseas.

I know you and Mrs. Bradford are
concerned about the commodore. I
am looking after him as well as I am
able to. He is the kindest, most under
standing man I have ever known, and
these past weeks he has become like a
second father to me. His forbearance
is remarkable, considering that we
have to contend with a most difficult
skipper—a hillbilly who has learned to
speak passable English in Navy
schools. He is a brilliant seaman and
excellent navigator but every now and
then reverts to type, erupting in the
coarsest backwoods language I've

ever heard. We are coping.
Now for the difficult part.
If I tell you that I was hoping you
would not write to me you would
think me rude. Nonetheless, it is so.
Yes, our time together was exciting.
But your sudden emergence in my life
poses questions I must resolve. I
know the above sentences may puzzle
you but I will say no more for now.
This stint overseas will give me the
opportunity to sort things out.

Liam

With Nora's letter out of the way he could con-
centrate on his father's message. He slit open the en-
velope with a penknife.

Dear Liam,

I haven't any idea when this letter will
get to you, but I want to tell you that
we all miss you terribly already. San
Francisco is full of sailors these days
and every time I see a naval officer I
think of you. Things are going as always in Sacramento. Politicians are
politicians and they can be awful
bores We are all praying for your
safe return. I have spoken to Father
Stamler and he prays for you, too.
I would be less than honest if I did not
tell you that in my heart I am hoping
your naval service will have a
positive effect on you, that you can
forget past indiscretions and find
your true self.

Love,
Dad

***

In his cabin, Bradford eagerly tore open the letter from his wife. He read it searching for assurance that there was a way out of their dilemma and that her ultimatum was not really her final word.

>
> Dearest Lover:
>
> I pray this letter finds you in good spirits. As for me, I am as well as I can be without having you nearby. Nora has returned to school and it is quiet here. Mildred tries to keep my spirits up (she is a dear!). The only visitor we have is Mr. Ritter who comes by every so often.
> Charles, you know I love you. But I would be lying to you if I did not re peat that I cannot go on with this marriage if you remain an infrequent visitor from the Navy. Please take care of yourself.
>
> I love you with all my heart,
>
> June

There was a short letter from Nora, too.

>
> Dear Dad:
>
> Miss you. Come home soon. Take good care. One favor: If Liam says anything about me please tell me. I want to know his opinion.

Right now, I've only
time for a note. I will
write you a longer let-
ter later today.

If you need anything
write and let us know.

Love,
Nora

Chapter X

When the *1525* reached Plymouth, Royal Navy Admiral Romney sent a car to pick up Bradford, Liam, and Cadgett, even though they could have used an American Navy jeep.

The three of them were waiting at the foot of the gangway when the English Ford drove up. The driver, leaped from the car, and saluted smartly, then opened the passenger door for the American officers.

"How far is it to the admiral's headquarters?" Bradford asked.

"A few miles north of the city, sir."

"About ten miles altogether?"

"Yes, sir."

The three American naval officers were driven through blitz-battered Plymouth on roads nearly void of civilian traffic. Often they had to pass around slow driving American military traffic with their "Left Wheel Drive" warning stenciled on the back end of the vehicles. There was also the occasional British military vehicle, smaller, less imposing.

In a little over half an hour, the Ford turned into a long driveway winding through an estate so well tended it could have passed for a golf course. Ahead was a large Georgian-style mansion.

"That's it, sir," the driver pointed out.

"The Brits sure are good to themselves," Liam whispered to Bradford.

"Well," Bradford replied, "it takes a lot of desks to plan an invasion."

"Of course," Liam said.

"The sentry will direct you to the admiral's office," the driver said after he opened the door and sa-

"Thank you," Bradford said.

The drive looked pleased at being thankful.

On their way up the path to the entrance Bradford said, "My conversation with Romney will be confidential. While I'm with him, you can get our orders."

"Aye aye, sir," Liam said and asked directions from the sentry while Cadgett stood quietly by.

"Admiral Romney's office is through that door there, sir, then the last door on the left," Liam related to Bradford.

"Wait here for me if you finish first," Bradford instructed to Liam and Cadgett.

"Aye aye, sir," said Liam.

Cadgett remained silent.

***

He was so tall, he had been called "Lofty" when he was a junior officer. His high coloring, gunmetal-gray hair and elevated jaw marked him as close to a storybook British admiral as they come.

On being told that Bradford had arrived, Romney left his office and walked quickly to meet his visitor. They shook hands vigorously.

"Charles, you old sea dog, I heard you were in command of the flotilla that came in today."

"It's good to see you again, George," he said with a spreading smile, and followed Romney into his office.

"Sit down, Charles," Romney told him. "Your showing up here is one of those pleasant little surprises life has for us."

"Last time I saw you, George, was 1941. We were drinking pilfered rum below decks on *Augusta* in Placentia Bay."

Romney leaned back in his chair and Bradford heard it creak; it was an old chair, a retread. In fact, the entire office was furnished that way: scraped together odds and ends, repaired seating and repainted desks. Only the photograph on the wall of King George was new.

The poor bastards are worn out at the elbows,

114

Bradford thought.

Romney followed up Bradford's remark about Placentia Bay.

"With Churchill and Roosevelt and their staffs making all those momentous decisions, there was nothing left for us lowly ships' officers to do but mischief."

Bradford did not speak for several moments. Neither did Romney. It was as if they were both thinking about the good times that were. Then broached an unpleasant subject. "Sorry about *Prince of Wales*. It shouldn't have happened."

"Yes," Romney answered. "They never should have sent out battleships without air cover. God knows Pearl Harbor ought to have been lesson enough. Lost a lot of friends. I was lucky. I'd been transferred just before she sailed to Singapore."

Romney fell silent again, then brightened. "Your old ship's still around. Matter of fact *Augusta*'s in Southampton."

"Another of life's happy coincidences," Bradford said.

Romney nodded and ducked his head, reaching for a low drawer in his desk. Soon, he came up smiling.

"Bourbon. Only Yank generals have it these days."

Without asking, Romney poured Bradford three fingers of whiskey in a glass he kept on his desk, then did the same for himself.

"Cheers!" Romney toasted.

"Cheers!" Bradford echoed.

"Confusion to our enemies."

"Amen."

They both drank, Bradford with relish and Romney with careful sips, as if the bourbon were a rare wine.

Bradford and Romney both sat back and enjoyed the whiskey's effect.

"We lost two vessels on the way over," Bradford said mournfully.

"Rotten luck. Thank goodness they weren't LSTs. It's not known outside of SHAEF and the Admiralty, but because of a shortage of LSTs two operations have had to be delayed."

"Two?"

"D-day by a month. The Mediterranean operation by two. Not enough landing craft for simultaneous landings."

"Things that critical? Separating the two will make each less effective."

"Know what Churchill said when we told him?" Romney asked.

He began to speak in a bad imitation of Churchill, "The fate of two great empires is tied to some goddamn things called LSTs."

Bradford smiled with satisfaction. He was gratified to discover that the importance of his command was known in the highest government circles.

"Was the second empire France or was that a sarcastic reference to the United States?" Bradford asked.

"We mused about that. The old man can be enigmatic."

Bradford took a breath and said, "What now, George?"

"Three of your LSTs to Brixham. Five stay here in Plymouth. They'll load combat engineers from one of your infantry divisions. We're to have a dress rehearsal. A spot like the French beachhead: Strangull Strand."

"Ugly name for a bloodless exercise."

"Bloodless, we hope."

"Oh?"

"Nothing to keep you up nights."

"Come on, George."

"There's been Jerry MTB action there in the past."

"E-boats?"

"Yes."

Bradford had been briefed about the German *Schnellbootwaffe* in Washington. Their motor torpedo boats were faster than both the British and

American boats of the same type. They carried two torpedoes in their tubes and two in reserve, plus a 40mm and a 37mm gun. Besides their superior speed, they were designed to not throw up a rooster tail while cutting through the water, so they were difficult to see coming as well as going.

"When?" Bradford asked.

"Three weeks from now. April twenty-seven and twenty eight. Your chaps up to it?"

"We could make the invasion without a rehearsal. But that doesn't mean we can't use the practice to iron out a kink or two."

Romney got up and walked to a chest on the far side of his office. He pulled open a drawer and removed a chart.

"Here's one of our charts of the area. It's probably a trifle more up-to-date than yours. We have nearly a month to study the exercise. There'll be other meetings. Plenty of time to get your questions answered."

Romney replaced the bourbon in the drawer. He sipped his drink, then placed his glass back on the desk.

"Beautiful color, bourbon," he said looking at the whiskey left in the glass, the light from the desk lamp behind it.

"How much danger?"

"A few months ago, even a few weeks ago I would have said *much*. But with D-day imminent, we've increased our destroyer screen between England and the Continent. Our radar is wide-eyed, and we have a special unit set up just to watch Jerry's E-boats." Romney got to his feet. "I'll show you out."

They walked to the door. Romney put his hand on Bradford's shoulder.

"One more thing," Romney said when they had reached the door. "If you're attacked, stop for nothing. Not even survivors. Get to the nearest English port as fast as those LSTs can move."

"I understand," said Bradford.

"We can't afford to lose even one LST. Expect Admirals Keller and Calvert to stress that when they

117

bigot you tomorrow."

"Bigot?"

"Those who have been let in on the invasion plan."

"Thank for the briefing, George."

"As you fellows say, have fun."

Chapter XI

On his way out of the Admiral Romney's headquarters Cadgett caught his first glimpse of Claudia Wakefield. His attention was caught by a small hand guiding an eraser rubbing out an error on a page in a typewriter roller. The British Navy Wren held her head only inches from the machine, her jade eyes showing gentle annoyance. The sun entering from the window liquefied her pale blonde hair. There was something about her that was mysteriously familiar to him, but there was also a softness that differentiated her from the girls he had known back home. Cadgett stopped and stared, and when she pouted, his mouth went dry.

Cadgett watched her finish her correction and noticed her glance up to meet his stare. Her face flushed crimson. Reacting to her embarrassment, he left hastily. During the trip back to Plymouth, Cadgett seemed agitated.

"What's wrong?" Bradford asked.

"Wait until we're back aboard," Cadgett answered and motioned toward the driver.

"I see," Bradford's said and his eyebrows crinkled with concern.

After they were dropped off, his story poured out of Cadgett. "I stopped at the American section. Admiral Lundy's staff. I asked them for escort orders. They had none for us. Fitzpatrick asked the Brits for communication plans. They had none. Every question we had, they

119

told us we did not have to know that. Everything we had to know would be in our Operation Orders."

"I'm sure there's good reason...."

"Good reason, hell!" Cadgett said. "They're getting ops together for Overlord. Commodore, we have been downgraded in priority."

"Nonsense."

"They treated us as if we were a nuisance," Liam chimed in. "Couldn't be bothered with trivialities like our exercise."

"I'm afraid your Irish prejudice is showing, Liam. Let me tell you something...."

The commodore straightened himself to a taller height. His eyes reflected his seriousness. "The Brits have been at this game a lot longer than we have. They know their enemy. They know what they're doing. Their naval tradition goes back to before American was even a word. They're no fools—no fools."

"That's just it, Commodore," Cadgett said. They know their enemy. And they're so used to being whipped by him that they've learned to take it. They're relaxed. They drop everything for tea. They stand around playing grab ass. They know they'll win in the end because we're here now and they're satisfied with that."

"Know what I heard back there?" Liam added. "Some British units rioted when told they were going into the beaches early. They're just back from North Africa and say it's someone else's turn to spearhead."

"So much for British stiff upper lips," Cadgett commented and chuckled perversely.

Bradford said, "The Brits will do their part and they'll do it with surpassing bravery."

"Of course, sir," Liam said.

Now Bradford reverted to his true height and moved back. He smiled and put his arm around Liam's shoulder. "Don't worry. It'll turn out all right."

***

120

British Naval headquarters was uncommonly busy. Navy people, men and women, were typing, filing, printing and delivering mountains of detailed instructions to every naval unit that was to have a role in the coming invasion. The heightened activities shortened tempers and people were not as civil to one another as during the calmer days of the preceding winter.

At her desk, Claudia Wakefield, one of the most reliable ratings on the headquarters staff, was beginning to flag. She had been at it since early morning and here it was 4 p.m. and no relief in sight.

An occasional American officer passed by and tried to chat with her . Claudia had been on dates with a few American officers who had come to the headquarters on business. She had found them not as worldly as their British counterparts, but attractively self-confident and singularly well groomed. Despite their reputations as tireless womanizers, few ever tried to get beyond a few kisses. It was her manner that put them off. She appeared to them pristine, a gift of great value to be unwrapped only on invitation.

Lieutenant Dobson, her unit chief, approached with a sneer on his face. "You know that pushy Yank who was in here yesterday trying to get to the front of the queue?"

Claudia took her fingers off the keys and nodded.

"A paddy name, Fitz something. Oh, here it is, Fitzpatrick," Dobson read after running his fingers over the list of those to receive copies. "It's the monitoring frequency he was asking for, the one for convoy M-9, Exercise Mongoose they're calling it. Just type it in. It won't take a moment."

"Put it down here, sir," Claudia said pointing to a clear spot on her desk, "I'll have it for you as soon as I finish this."

"Thanks, Luv," Dobson said, set the sheet down and dashed off to another task.

Claudia sped through the job before her, then laid it aside, then started on the task Dobson had assigned her. She had typed the first numeral, on Liam's copy when she was interrupted by Priscilla Evans.

"Here's your tea, Claudia." Priscilla moved to place the cup and saucer squarely on Lieutenant Dobson's hand-written note.

The tea wobbled in Priscilla's hand when she set it down. The liquid sloshed in the cup, spilling over into the saucer. There already was some tea in the saucer had not been blotted up and the added liquid that caused it to overflow onto Dobson's note. The tea spread to the numbers, mixed with the ink and blurred the numerals.

"Look what you've done!" Claudia cried, and grabbed a handkerchief from her pocket and vainly attempted to repair the damage.

"I'm frightfully sorry," Priscilla Evans apologized. "Here, let me help you." Priscilla got her handkerchief from her pocket and went after the wet stain.

"Never mind," Claudia pushed Priscilla's hand away. "I'll manage better without your help."

"Goodness," Priscilla pouted, "I said I was sorry. You don't have to bite my head off."

"Please, Priscilla, I'll take care of it!"

Priscilla Evans, offended by the impatient attitude of the usually tolerant Claudia Wakefield, stalked off in high dudgeon.

"Silly sod," Claudia muttered under her breath. Claudia was furious to find the tea had made the numbers run. They had become a soggy blur.

"Oh, bullocks!" she exclaimed. "Well, no real harm done. I remember the numbers."

Near exhaustion, nerves frayed by Priscilla Evan's clumsiness, Claudia typed in the number her memory dictated. It was one digit off.

***

Cadgett knew the invasion was just days off. He could tell by the radio traffic, by the increased pace of personnel ashore, and by the kind of supplies coming aboard. If he were to see the British Wren again it would have to be now.

Cadgett's first step was to inquire whether he could absent himself from his ship for one day. The operations officer at American naval headquarters pondered Cadgett's request for several moments.

"I suppose it will be all right."

"Nothing will come off while I'm gone?"

"No."

"You're sure?"

"We have plenty of time."

"Any chance of borrowing a jeep?"

"Sorry. We're short of vehicles as it is."

Getting to British naval headquarters proved to be no problem. Cadgett positioned himself on the main road leading out of the city and flagged down the first vehicle that came along. The soldier at the wheel of what the British called a "tender," was eager for company. "Hop in, Yank," he said.

"Thanks."

"Where are you going?" the soldier asked.

"Ten or so miles straight ahead."

"You're in luck, mate. I'm going that far."

Cadgett had hardly settled in when the soldier tried to start a conversation.

"Looks like the big show's coming off soon," he commented.

"I don't know," Cadgett answered.

"On my way here I noticed a lot of troops shifting about."

"They're always shifting them."

"Not like this."

The soldier understood from Cadgett's laconic replies that he did not wish to gossip about military matter.

"On official business?" the soldier paused. "Of course not. You wouldn't be out catching a ride if you were."

"Right. It's private."

"A girl?"

Cadgett did not answer, and the soldier took that as affirmative.

"You chaps do well with our girls."

"Do we?"

"It's a good thing, I say. Marry them. Clear the trash out of our country."

Cadgett turned to look at the grinning Englishman. He reached out and grabbed the top of the man's shoulder with his big hand and squeezed. The driver's eyes bulged with terror and he almost lost control of the truck.

"What the bloody hell are you doing?" the soldier gurgled through a constricted throat.

"Listen, asshole," Cadgett snarled. "You just drive this truck, hear? And take that shit-eating grin off your ugly face or I'll rip it off and have it mailed to your mother."

"Let go or we'll crash."

"If we do crash I'll make sure your death looks like it happened in the accident, hear?"

"Let go, Yank, let go!"

Cadgett released the pressure and slowly removed his hand.

"It was just a joke," the soldier said.

"I got no sense of humor," Cadgett answered.

"Sorry," the man said weakly, and went silent. Some minutes later he slowed the truck.

"That it?" The soldier asked.

"Yeah, stop over yonder."

When the truck came to a halt, the soldier leaped out, opened the passenger side door for Cadgett, then climbed back in the truck and started it rolling. He shouted out the window to Cadgett,

"We bomb Germany by night and that's harder."

With that the soldier stomped on the accelerator and sped off.

Cadgett went to the room in headquarters where he had seen the Englishwoman. He walked inside as if on business. There were enough American naval officers walking in and out for no one to question him. For a moment he was afraid she was off duty and his trip was in vain. Then he spied her at her desk organizing a sheaf of papers she had just finished typing, and it was as if a hot wind flashed through his body. Cadgett's throat locked.

Cadgett composed himself, then walked out of the headquarters building and onto a company street. There he stationed himself at the door of a Nissen hut and waited. He would wait until morning if necessary, but he would speak to her.

It began to rain, lightly at first, then harder, pelting down in large globules. Cadgett had not brought a raincoat with him. Unused to the vagaries of English weather, he was caught by surprise. He fled across the road to a cook house and took up his watch in the doorway, partially sheltered from the rain.

It was almost two hours before Claudia Wakefield emerged from the hut along with two of her fellow Wrens. They looked up at the sky, donned their raincoats, and began to walk up the company street.

Cadgett stepped from the cook house door and confronted the trio. The Navy women drew back in surprise, but then Claudia recognized him.

"Oh, it's you," Claudia blurted out, and a blush began at her cheeks and spread down her neck.

"I want to talk," Cadgett said.

Claudia looked at him, then at her friends.

"It's all right," one of them said. "We'll see you back at the hut."

With that, the two Royal navy women hurried off.

Claudia and Cadgett did not seek shelter; they stood on the softening earth and stared at each other.

"You remembered me," Cadgett said.

"Yes, I noticed you looking at me the other day."

"I'm sorry if I made you uncomfortable."

"You did."

"Why?"

"I don't know."

Cadgett hesitated. He feared his request would be rejected. If so, he would settle for being in her presence for a little while longer.

"Can we go somewhere and chat?" he asked finally. He deliberately chose the word "chat," more commonly used in England than America, hoping it would make him appear less threatening.

Claudia hesitated.

"You can leave whenever you want," he said. "I won't even ask why."

"All right," she said.

"Where?" he asked.

"There's a NAAFI just over the road."

"Lead the way," Cadgett said, scarcely able to conceal his relief.

Soon after Cadgett and Claudia began their walk to the small cottage the British had converted into a coffee house for servicemen, it stopped raining. The sun glared white behind a haze of thinning, dark gray clouds. Under their feet the soil had turned to mud and it stuck to their shoes and slowed their pace. Cadgett and Claudia entered the NAAFI after first scraping the mud off their shoes with leaves they plucked from a nearby bush. Inside, they each chose a sandwich of paper thin brown bread with margarine and, to Cadgett, unidentifiable greens.

"You must have thought about me," he said, after sitting down at one of the tables.

"Why do you say that?" she asked.

"You remembered me. That took thought."

He drank his tea in silence.

"Aren't you eating your sandwich?" she asked him.

"Not much of a sandwich," he replied.

"Yes, well, we've had a difficult time."

"I didn't mean to criticize," he apologized, but left it uneaten.

She looked at him and shuddered.

"Cold?" he asked.

"No."

"You trembled."

Cadgett reached over and took Claudia's hand and felt it go hot under his touch. When she did not withdraw it, he increased the pressure.

"What's your name?

She smiled, took control of her hand back from him, and leaned away just far enough not to signal rejection.

"Claudia Wakefield. Yorkshire."

"Verne Cadgett. Kentucky."

126

He paused. "What's your family like?"

"Only child. Mother dead. Father teaches at the University. Nothing much more to tell."

He stared at her eyes. He had never before seen eyes like hers. They were dark green, dense, almost mineral-like in their opaqueness.

"You're looking at my eyes."

"They're right pretty."

"Oh, you Yanks!"

The way she said it was so endearing, he could not resist laughing.

"You think I'm just a horny Yank?"

"Horny?"

"Yes. On the make."

"Oh, randy."

"Yeah, randy."

"Yes, I do."

Cadgett reacted with embarrassment. It was hard for him to think of himself as a womanizer. In fact, he had not gone near a woman since Cora Lee had been killed. He wondered if he was telegraphing a frantic sexual message. "Do I give that impression?"

"I sense something."

"What?"

"I don't know," she said. "A,a,a smoldering? No, that's the wrong word."

"It's as good as any other. I know what you mean."

Cadgett paused, drank some tea, and continued to ignore the sandwich on the table in front of him. "I've been...ah...well, kind of restless since I first saw you," he said. "That's all I can say about it."

"You want to make love to me, then bugger off?"

"I want to make love to you and stay."

"I don't believe you, of course. It's a flattering offer, but...."

"But what?"

"It would complicate things."

"Complicate?"

"Suppose we fall in love. And then you have to leave. Neither of us knows if you'll return."

"From the invasion?"

127

"Yes."

"I'd have thought you would think the opposite. You'll make love to me because I may not return."

"I think differently. It's always been a problem."

Cadgett sensed he could persuade her. He fought to suppress a burning inside of him. It was painful to look at her and not reach out to touch her, to run his hand over her cheek, to kiss her shoulders and her breasts.

"I want to make love to you today. Now. But I respect your reasoning. I will do anything you ask of me."

Claudia placed her hand on her breast and caught her breath. "Are you sure?"

"I'm sure because it's the way you want it."

"All right, then, shall we go back?"

"Yes, it's almost dark."

***

"My goodness," Claudia said when she saw Cadgett waiting for her at the entrance to her hut a week later. "I didn't expect you'd be back so soon."

"I tried to get in touch with you by phone," he explained, "but there was no way I could get through."

"Security. They've tightened it recently."

"I'll be off somewhere soon. I wanted to see you before I left. You know. Never can tell."

"Let's go," she said, "I'm off duty."

"Not tea again?"

"Of course," she said, hooked her arm into his and pulled him along, pretending he was going reluctantly.

The NAAFI was crowded and they had to wait for a table. They held hands, and she was pleased. There was a strength in his touch, which was hard, and overpoweringly masculine. She went moist inside and was astonished at her reaction.

He's just a man, she told herself but she knew he was more than that to her. He was some half-forgotten libidinous dream of her adolescence.

They drank tea and watched the British service

men and women come and go.

"Come on," she said. "Try the sandwich."

"Margarine and what? Lettuce?"

"Call it what you will. There's nowhere else to eat around here. You'll die of hunger."

Cadgett cautiously took a small bite.

"Well?"

"Tastes like...uh...margarine and grass. Seriously, it's not bad." He wolfed down the rest of it.

"I think I know where you're going," Claudia told him.

"Then you know I won't be gone long -- if I'm lucky."

When she first met him she could sense that he desired her so much he could scarcely contain himself. Now his excitement had spread to her like a virulent contagion.

"I have been thinking about you, Verne," she whispered, and regretted the words the moment she uttered them. How could she be so forward, so reckless?

He reacted grimly, almost reluctantly. "I haven't stopped thinking about you for a moment since I first saw you."

"What kind of thinking?"

"Oh, you know, kids' stuff. I'm stroking your cheeks, kissing you lightly on the lips, inhaling your scent."

Claudia felt herself go red in the face and her cheeks began to burn.

"I'm afraid mine aren't as romantically indirect."

"How do you mean?" he questioned.

"Mine are embarrassingly lascivious."

The word "lascivious," a word he had read but never heard spoken, delayed his reply for a moment, then he said, "That's not bad news."

She paused, thinking, weighing an approach that would not make her seem glib as a tart. "I can get away for a few days. They've been trying to get me to take some unused leave I'm owed. They said I can have it anytime I liked."

"I take it then you've changed your mind," Cadgett

said with a catch in his throat.

"Yes, I hope you haven't changed yours."

"I'm not needed for a few days myself, he said. I can slip around."

"Slip around?"

"What you and I will be doing for the next few days."

"How about slipping around to a small village in Cornwall I used to go to on holiday. St. Maude. It's just across the bay from Falmouth. Nobody will bother us there."

"Sounds good."

"We'll take the train from Plymouth. We can get a coach in Truro."

"Horses?"

"A big motor car with lots of seats."

"A bus, for Christ's sake. Why don't you say so."

She laughed and returned his teasing in kind. "Now, look, Verne. If you're going to poke fun at my English, I put you on notice, yours is much more vulnerable."

"Let's go to Plymouth," he said.

***

After stopping at her hut to pack a small bag and convince her superiors she could immediately take the leave she was owed, Cadgett and Claudia walked the short distance to the train to Truro. Claudia went to sleep on his shoulder the moment they settled into their seats. She was breathing gently on his neck. He turned his face toward her and inhaled. Her scent was sweet to him, like a mild liqueur. He grew dizzy with the pleasure of it. His body tingled with a sensation more than sexual. Then he, too, fell asleep. They woke upon their arrival in Truro, and after a short wait boarded the bus for St. Maude.

The village lay at the bottom of a hill on a shallow inlet poking into the belly of Cornwall from Falmouth Bay. Visitors entered the tiny town of fifty or so 17th and 18th century houses after rolling down a steep hill. The road led to a cobblestone street that faced the waterfront where stood a stone quay and a small building that used to serve as a toll house. Two small hotels looked out on the street, a general store, and a comfortable pub, the Quarter Moon. An arc of hills embraced the village. To the south a few houses showed through the greenery of a hillside beyond which a visitor could glimpse a crumbling Tudor castle. In a vale to the west was a Norman church, and behind it an ancient graveyard with eroded tombstones protruding from the earth like damaged teeth.

The moment they stepped from the bus, Claudia's eyes shone. She grabbed Cadgett's elbow with one hand and, carrying her overnight bag with the other, rushed up the street.

"There it is. The Brigantine, the hotel we used to stay at when I was a girl."

He caught her enthusiasm and rushed with her to the hotel entrance. They opened the door to a sight of near devastation.

"It's empty," she gasped.

"Nobody's cleaned this place for weeks," he commented.

"It's so sad," she exclaimed as they walked past the dusty reservation desk into what used to be the dining room.

"Double racks," he remarked and walked to the first of twenty or so two-tiered steel bunks. "They must have billeted soldiers here."

"Yes," she muttered and turned to leave.

On the street, they stopped a passing townswoman and inquired about the hotel.

"The Brigantine? Oh, they closed that down in 1941. Our boys occupied it for years. They manned those rusting old gun mounts over near the water when we thought we were going to be invaded. Then it was Yank soldiers, and most recently Yank sailors. They left in their little boats about a fortnight ago. Nice boys. Never gave us a bit of trouble."

"The other hotel in the same condition?" Claudia inquired.

"Worse, I'm afraid. Did you used to spend holidays here?"

"Yes."

"You will again. There's a NAAFI over the road. Go have yourselves a nice cup of tea. If you mean to stay for a while, I can direct you to Mary Penrose. She'll be glad to put you up. Bed and Breakfast kind of thing."

Cadgett asked, "How do we find her?"

"Fourth house up that street," she told them pointing to a narrow lane.

"Much obliged," Cadgett replied.

Before calling on Mrs. Penrose, Claudia and Cadgett stopped at the NAAFI.

"You wait here," he said. "I'm going to the store over yonder and buy some toilet articles."

"I have enough for us both."

"A razor and shaving cream, too?"

"Yes, but not the kind that would suit you, I suppose."

"Be right back," he said, left the NAAFI and walked to the store.

"Good morning," greeted a stout middle-aged woman with graying red hair.

"Need a razor and shaving cream,"

"We can accommodate you." The woman turned to fill Cadgett's order from the shelf behind her. "You're not one of the Yanks who were here recently, are you?" she asked when she turned to him again.

"No."

She lay what he asked for on the counter and collected his payment. "Good to see a Yank here again."

"Thanks," Cadgett said. "Nice to be here."

***

Cadgett returned to the NAAFI, and collected Claudia. They walked up the street and knocked on the door of the house to which they had been directed.

"Mrs. Penrose?" Claudia said after the door opened to reveal a slight, dark haired, Cornish coun-

132

trywoman with an incredulous mouth and cynical eyes.

"Yes?" Mrs. Penrose said. She inspected the both of them and a knowing look glinted in her eyes. "Is it a room you want?"

"Yes."

"For how long? Because if it's for a quick roll on my sheets, you've the wrong place. I'm not running a brothel."

"Oh, no," Claudia objected, her face reddening. "We're on holiday. Three days."

"You're married then?" Mrs. Penrose asked. "Don't answer that. I can't abide lies. Come on in, children. I'll give you a cup of tea and we'll talk business."

Claudia and Cadgett glanced at each other and smiled.

They sat down at the table in the tiny kitchen while Mrs. Penrose put on the kettle. Then she took a chair across from them.

"I'll put it to you straight," Mrs. Penrose said, almost defiantly. "I overcharge. A quid a day. Reason is that the place is small and it's a real inconvenience to have you. What's more, my husband, rest his soul, had a bathroom installed upstairs. That's rare around here. If one pound is too much, say so, and we'll all save time. I'll serve you the tea either way. Free."

"A pound is fine," Cadgett said.

"Don't be so hasty," Mrs. Penrose cautioned, "You haven't seen the room or heard my terms yet."

"I'm sure it will be fine."

"All right," she conceded. "Take it sight unseen if that's your wish."

Mrs. Penrose removed the kettle from the stove and poured the tea, which was hotter than at the NAAFI and better tasting too.

"Good," Cadgett pronounced after sipping his tea.

Mrs. Penrose drank from her cup and eyed them suspiciously again.

"Where will you eat?" she asked.

"We never thought of it," Claudia admitted.

"No restaurants here. You can take the ferry to

Falmouth, but going there and return twice a day will take all your time. You can have your meals here if you wish. Another quid a day."

"Sounds fine," Claudia said.

"That will be okay," Cadgett said, and smiled at how reasonable the prices were.

"One more thing before money changes hands," Mrs. Penrose continued. "This is a small house. You can hear every creak of a bedspring, every break of wind. I require you wait until I'm out before making love. I'm an old woman and I've done my share of rogering, but still, it's embarrassing to hear all those grunts and groans. Now, I'm out for most of the day doing sewing here and there. I hope you can save it till then. Agreed?"

"Agreed," Cadgett replied, "except we would like you to leave for a couple of hours today. Just to begin with."

Mrs. Penrose smiled for the first time, revealing absent teeth and neglected gums.

"Can't wait, eh? All right, then, that will be acceptable. I have a thing or two to do anyway. That'll be six quid in advance and your room's the first door on your left, the top of the stairs. The linen's clean. Just washed the other day. Towels in the chest. I sleep in the other bedroom."

Cadgett reached into his pocket and removed his billfold. "Here you are," he said. He pushed the pound notes across the table.

"I'll pay half," Claudia interrupted reaching into her pocket.

"The hell you say," Cadgett said and restrained her with a quick hand.

Mrs. Penrose, the glow of new found wealth in her eyes, scooped up the pound notes and retreated to the door.

"Now, don't break my bedsprings," she cackled, and winked as she left.

"Let's go upstairs," Claudia whispered with a catch in her throat.

"Can't wait." Cadgett came to her quickly and eased her to the kitchen floor.

With a desire so fierce it stripped her of the deepest inhibition and restraint. Claudia jerked up her skirt and tugged at her undergarments.

Cadgett grabbed and pulled, stripping them from her body. Without taking the time to undress, he unbuttoned his pants.

She squeaked with pain when he penetrated her, but soon she was urging him on.

A pink rash erupted above her breasts and spread to her shoulders.

Reviving, she heard him say, "I'm sorry I finished so soon."

"It was good." Claudia assured him.

They lay on the floor together regaining their strength. After a while, when their breathing had evened, he said,"It's not very comfortable on the floor. Let's go upstairs."

Cadgett helped Claudia rise and they mounted the creaking, lopsided stairs to their room. To her surprise the room was lovely. There were whitewashed walls, a fireplace, a large old fashioned four-poster bed, a dresser, a lampstand, and a chest of drawers. Nothing was later than Queen Victoria's early reigning years. The smell was delicious, clean and fresh.

No doubt about it. Mrs. Penrose was an excellent housekeeper. Claudia set her grip on the floor and Cadgett laid his just-purchased toilet articles on the dresser.

Now Claudia undressed and stood before him waiting while he stripped off his uniform. Cadgett was struck by her body. It was not salaciously ample but small, and attractively proportioned. He eased her down on the bed, and made love to her again.

"No more," she said.

Afterwards, he lay beside her. They kissed gently on the lips, their reservoir of passion empty.

Afterwards, he bathed, but not before complaining about the absence of a shower.

"You Yanks," Claudia teased.

***

135

As he shaved she could hear him sing snatches of strange ditties, something about a big speckled bird.

How unEnglish the lyrics sounded. Yet he was descended from Britons. There was a certain spirit of the hills in these songs that she found alien. Perhaps their attitude originated in Scotland or Ulster. She did not know.

***

"My goodness," Claudia exclaimed after Mrs. Penrose had placed their breakfast on the table and left. "Wonder where she got the eggs?"

"What do you call these?" Cadgett asked turning over something that resembled American frankfurters, but that were fatter and paler in color.

"Bangers, Verne, try them."

He lopped off a slice and tasted it.

"Good?" she asked.

"I won't say good, but it's no worse than what we serve our sailors for Sunday lunch."

"You call them bangers as well?"

"Horsecock is what we call it."

"I must say," she giggled, "you've lent the language some color."

They attacked their food, devouring their eggs and bangers and several slices of toast smeared with orange marmalade.

"She has a secret source of supply, that woman has," Claudia said. "I doubt if she's come by this food honestly."

"Country people always find a way."

Claudia looked across the table at him and laid a hand on his.

"Let's walk," she suggested. "I want to try that steep hill we came down into the village."

They left the house and walked to the square, passing the public telephone booth just outside the NAAFI.

136

"I'm tempted to call my father," she told him.

"Go ahead," Cadgett said.

"I wrote to him about you."

"You couldn't have had much to say."

"You don't know women very well. We can spend an hour with a man and write a book about him the length of *War and Peace.*

"Here are some coins, give him a call."

"All right," Claudia agreed, entered the phone booth and placed her trunk call.

A deep voice answered the ring with a clipped "Hello."

"How are you, father?"

"Fine, lass."

"I'm glad to know you're well."

"How are you, dear?"

"Fine. I'm in St. Maude on a three day holiday."

"St. Maude?"

"St. Maude. It's changed. It's sad to see the Brigantine closed. And so many of the townfolk are gone. Not a young man in sight. All in the services. Remember the Yank naval officer I wrote to you about? No, the younger one. He's right here. Want to talk to him?"

"All right."

She handed the receiver to Cadgett and said, "Here. Say a few words."

"How you doing?" Cadgett said.

"Pardon me?" the voice of Mr. Wakefield came.

"How are you?"

"Excuse me?"

"Hello. How are you?"

"What?"

"I'm sorry." Cadgett handed the receiver to Claudia. "He doesn't seem to understand me. Must be the accent."

Claudia laughed and seized the phone.

"What happened? Oh, couldn't understand. You would if you were here in person. The phone does something to the highs or lows or something. Yes, I'll call you when I get back to Plymouth. Yes.

Goodbye."

Cadgett and Claudia walked down the street, past the NAAFI, and up to the foot of the hill. Holding hands, they went forward, purposefully as soldiers on the march.

"Why, you're puffing already," Claudia said. "We're not halfway up yet."

"You're in better shape than I am. We don't get much exercise aboard ship."

"You best me in other physical activities, though," she remarked shyly.

It took him a moment to catch her meaning. "Well, it's been a long time."

She reached out and grabbed his hand as if to help him along. "I don't know a thing about you, Captain Cadgett."

"Well," he said, "I'll be glad to tell you when we reach the top."

"Come on, sailor," Claudia urged, and ran all the rest of the way.

Cadgett followed. When he arrived at the crest of the hill, he sat down in the grass along the east-west highway that crossed the road that led up the hill.

Claudia sank down beside him and looked at him with mock pity. "Poor thing. How will we win the war with winded allies?"

"Don't rub it in." He took out a cigarette and lighted it, then he motioned to her, asking if she'd like one.

She declined with a shake of her head. "Someone's coming."

A small, bent figure approached, which turned into an aged country woman pulling a barrow. In the barrow were pots of flowers: Canterbury bells, larkspurs, lupines, columbines, and more.

"Would you like flowers for our room?" Cadgett asked.

"Yes."

"How much for the entire barrow?"

"For the lot?" the old lady queried through a toothless mouth.

"What in the world are you doing?" Claudia

138

asked.

"I want to buy them all. She can go home then. Take the day off."

The crone shook her head emphasizing a shrunken face, eyes hidden by folds of skin, and sparse gray hair.

"Sorry, sir, but no, sir."

"Why not?"

"No, sir."

"All right then, we'll take these," Cadgett said and reached into the barrow and removed a bouquet of columbines.

"Sixpence, sir."

"Here's a half crown," Cadgett offered.

"No thank you, sir. It's sixpence and that's what you shall pay."

"All right then, here's a sixpence."

"Thank you, sir," she told him and with a tug, then a pull, resumed her journey.

Cadgett looked puzzled. "I'll never understand you Limeys. I thought the whole idea was to sell out as quickly as possible."

"I suspect the whole idea for her is to enjoy bringing color into her neighbors' lives and to survive while she's at it."

Claudia grew quiet and stared up at giant white balloons of clouds hanging over Cornwall.

"Now, out with it," she ordered.

"You know enough, don't you?"

"Not at all."

"I can make it up and keep your respect or tell the truth and lose it."

"Oh, come off it. We English aren't the snobs people think we are."

"Well, now, I don't rightly know about that. What I hear about you folks..." He stopped to puff his cigarette.

Claudia placed her arm across his chest and put her mouth closer to his. "Out with it!"

"It's like this. My daddy was a miner. Hurt bad in a cave in. If he didn't make white lightning we'd all have starved to death."

"What on earth is white lightning?"

"Moonshine. Illegal whiskey."

Her brow wrinkled into furrows but she made no comment.

"I was the first one in my family to graduate from high school. My daddy wanted me to quit and work to help support the family, but my teacher talked him out of it. She told him I was the brightest child in the school. I could make something of myself if I at least finished high school. He finally agreed."

"You mean you never attended college, yet you're an officer? A skipper, at that."

"I got damned high marks on every test the Navy ever gave me. They tell me I'm one of the smartest hillbillies this side of the Blue Ridge mountains." Then he laughed at his exaggeration.

"You've got a lot to offer, Verne."

"I don't know about that," Cadgett said. "The Navy is probably best for me. I won't go back to Kentucky. That's for damned sure."

"It's a good career, is it?"

"I may get as far as a captain's rank. That's three ranks up. I'm only a lieutenant, a full lieutenant, but a lieutenant, nevertheless."

"No further than captain?"

"Not a chance. Wrong momma and daddy. Wrong everything."

Claudia rolled over on top of him and put her lips on his.

"If you're what hillbillies are like, I like them."

"It's dangerous to like more than one at a time, you know. We have a reputation for being fiercely jealous."

"Are you married?" she asked matter-of-factly.

"I used to be."

She looked at him with serious eyes. She was more interested now. She wanted to know more.

"Divorced?" she asked.

"No."

"Oh, my, you're going to tell me something terrible."

He reached out and touched her hair.

"She died. Killed. My daughter, too."

"Don't tell me how," she whispered.

"All right."

"What was she like?"

"Like me. We were almost kin. Maybe we were back aways. She was blonde. Different from you. Taller, more buxom, I think the word is. Not as pretty as you, but pretty enough."

Claudia thought for a while, chose a clover and picked it. She pulled one of its petals and let it fall to the ground.

"Even though I was a sailor and had heard everything, I was still like a teenager around her."

"You were serious."

"Acted stupid, though. She wouldn't sleep with me for weeks after we met. I told her, 'I love you but I can't marry you.'"

"That must have focused her attention." Claudia tore off another petal, put it in her mouth and chewed on it.

"It's embarrassing to think about now. I thought I was being very adult. I said, until we sleep together I can't marry you because I don't know whether or not we're suited. I can't live with a woman who just puts up with me."

"What did she say?"

"She said, "Okay, we'll have a trial marriage. Then she suggested we get married by a Chinese priest, or monk, or something. That way we'll be married, she told me. But if things don't turn out, it won't really be legal, and we can go on our way. We went to Chinatown. Found some Chinaman. It was weird, but did the trick."

Claudia let the last clover and its stem fall to the ground and disappear into the grass. "Did it work out?"

"Yes."

"I'm glad."

Claudia changed her position on the ground then turned over on her back. She stared at the sky.

"Anything wrong?"

141

"Oh, no."

"You look like you're angry."

"No. I'm not. Just normal jealousy."

"I didn't mean to do that to you."

"I know. What you said just made me wonder."

"Wonder what?"

She sat up abruptly and looked away embarrassed. "Did you, well, did you have it better with her?"

Cadgett frowned. "It was different," he said.

"You'd rather be with her."

"I couldn't make that choice. I needed her then. I need you now."

"I see."

"Let's stop this. It can lead to trouble."

"You're right. Kiss me then. Like you have to kiss me or die."

He placed his lips on hers. Not hard, but gently, barely touching them.

"I like that," she breathed.

He rolled over. "And you," he asked. "Are you married?"

"No. Never have been."

"Your first lover?"

"Oh, what an indiscreet question. I hate to answer it."

"You owe me."

"I suppose I do."

"Tell me, then."

She smiled. She began to tell him, matter-of-factly, without rancor, anger or bitterness.

It was before Claudia's mother died. Her family had gone to Portugal on holiday. She was fourteen, pretty and nubile. They occupied a rented house on the beach just north of Lisbon. Her mother and father left her in the house with a servant while they went to a nearby village to shop. The servant fell asleep and Claudia took that opportunity to walk on the beach. It started to drizzle and the few people on the beach left. She was alone. She took off her shoes and walked in the sand. It was good to be the only person in the world. She looked at the delicious, green

142

ocean and thought how wonderful it would be to take off all her clothes and swim in the surf.

Why not? she thought. There's no one else left in the world. She removed her clothes and splashed into the surf and through small waves into a quiet ocean. She swam happily, her head sprinkled with gentle rain every time she rose from the water. The sun came out, fiery orange and hot. She was tired now and turned toward the shore.

A Portuguese came across her thin, almost diaphanous smock and cotton panties on the sand. He picked up the panties and held them to his nose, inhaling the scent of them. He looked out to sea and saw Claudia swimming toward the shore. He knew she was naked; he held the evidence in his hand. He waited for her for a while, feeling himself beginning to swell. He considered the consequences, but his fear was buried under a landslide of desire. He hastily removed his clothes, squatted, and waited.

Coming up for air, Claudia saw the dark, naked figure on the beach. She stopped and began to tread water. She waited, terrified, until her strength gave out. Her choice was inescapable. She would have to swim to land or drown. In a last burst of strength, she flayed the ocean until she reached the shore, collapsed on the wet sand at the feet of the naked man. Breathing like an animal, he leaped upon her and turned her on her back. She was too exhausted to resist.

Later, she could not say it was lastingly traumatic. It was just something that happened to her.

"Well, we certainly have been honest with each other," she said after a pause.

"That's good, isn't it?"

"I don't know," she replied.

She lay in the grass her face clouded with concern. He watched her, wondering.

"What's wrong?" he asked.

"We're being honest with each other...."

"Yes."

"Then I should tell you this."

"What?"

143

"I've been seeing a man. Rather regularly. An American officer. I care for him."

"Care for him? What does that mean? You love him?"

"Not in the way you mean it."

"You're going to tell me you're just friends."

"More. But it's not what I have with you."

"Son of a bitch!" Cadgett exploded. He pushed Claudia aside and jumped to his feet.

"Don't be angry," she pleaded. "I was afraid this would happen," she added sadly.

He stood over her, glaring at the sky. He began to pace back and forth for a while, then he sat back down beside her.

"I know you weren't just sitting around waiting for me to show up. Still, it makes me crazy."

"Let's go back to the village," she pleaded.

She got her feet and brushed herself off. Bits of grass remained clinging to her uniform, detracting slightly from her usual immaculate appearance.

"All right, let's go back."

Cadgett and Claudia walked down the hill. This time they didn't hold hands. Cadgett seemed to her to be struggling with himself.

He walked beside her, still silent, still frowning. "Get rid of him," he growled.

"Excuse me?"

"Get rid of the guy."

"I can't, Verne, he's too good a friend."

"All right, then stop sleeping with him."

"I would, Verne, but it's too late. He would know something was wrong. He would take it as a rejection, that I no longer want his friendship."

"I don't give a rat's ass. Stop it."

Claudia did not reply.

They reached the bottom of the hill and walked up the street without speaking. When they arrived at the Quarter Moon, he insisted that they go inside.

The bartender, a Cornishman, squat as a fireplug, with hooded eyes and a blotched face, greeted them cordially.

"Pint," Claudia said.

"And you, sir?"

"Beer."

"We have no lager. And what we do have is warm by American standards. Damn little alcohol in it. War regulations."

"Shit!" Cadgett swore.

"Sorry, sir. Know how you feel about that. We had American soldiers and sailors here for a long time. They seldom drank here because of that."

"All right then, let's have some Scotch."

"Don't have any," the bartender answered, averting his eyes.

He left and began to draw Claudia's pint.

Cadgett looked around the pub. It was pleasing to him—all wood, the bar gleaming from a hundred years of polishing. He turned, his eyes on the bartender, as the man placed the foamless amber liquid in front of Claudia.

Cadgett's menacing silence began to make the bartender uncomfortable.

"How about a spot of gin instead, sir?" The bartender asked in a whisper.

"I'm for that," Cadgett answered. "Make it a triple."

The bartender looked at him quizzically, then reached under the bar and poured the drink where he would not be observed by his other customers.

Cadgett swallowed it all down in one gulp.

"Easy, there, Yank," the bartender cautioned. "Can't give you any more."

Cadgett slammed his empty whiskey glass on the bar. "Give me another," he demanded.

"I told you I can't, sir."

Cadgett reached into his pocket and came up with a five pound note. He threw it on the bar. "It this enough?"

"Oh, all right," the bartender relented, exasperated with the American.

The Cornishman reached under the bar and poured Cadgett another triple. After a quick look around, his arm shot out and placed the drink on the bar. Then it recoiled, deftly palming the note along

145

the way.

Cadgett drank the gin in three gulps, stood up and quietly waited for it to take effect. He did not have to wait long. The warmth coursed through his body and began to contact his consciousness.

"Let's go back to the house and fuck," Cadgett said.

Claudia slid off her chair and left the pub without a word.

"Barkeep! Barkeep!" Cadgett shouted, waving his empty glass at the man.

"No," the man refused, "and if you give me any trouble I'll call the constable."

"Oh, blow it out your ass," Cadgett cursed and walked out the door. He had almost reached Mrs. Penrose's house when the six gins hit him and he felt his legs liquefy. Still, he managed to find his way to the front door and let himself in.

He stumbled up the stairs, stopped in front of the door, composed himself and walked in without knocking.

Claudia was lying on the bed in her pre-war pajamas, staring red-eyed at the ceiling.

"Today didn't turn out too well, did it?" Cadgett slurred.

"No, it didn't."

"What do you expect? You want me to be happy sharing you with another guy."

"Verne, I'm afraid you'll never understand."

"What you really mean is that I'll never understand *you*."

"Take it as you wish."

Cadgett lunged at her, throwing himself across the bed and grabbing both her arms.

"Let go!" Claudia cried.

"Goddamn it! When Cora Lee died I thought I'd never find anyone who could replace her. Well, I did, and look what happens. My woman's screwing another guy."

"You're drunk," she announced with disgust in her voice and even more so, in her eyes. "Come on, go to bed. You need a good sleep."

"Don't shine me on." He squeezed her arms

146

tighter.

"Verne, please take your hands off. We'll talk about things like civilized people."

"Oh, I'm a savage, am I? Someone you have to remind to be civilized."

He lay down beside her and looked into her eyes. The green of them stirred him. What flashed through his mind whenever he looked into them was the same feeling he experienced at the first cool hint of a Kentucky autumn, or coming upon forest animals frisking near a creek on a quiet, peopleless morning.

Now her eyes showed a hint of fear, and he relented. He released her and lay back on his side of the bed.

"I suppose I should say I'm sorry," he said. "The truth is I have to be angry with you. It eases the pain."

"Verne, we've known each other for so short a time. Our attraction has been almost all physical."

"No..."

"Please, Verne, don't deny it. There hasn't been enough time to call it love."

"I don't care how short a time we know each other. I love you."

With that, the gin he had drunk put Cadgett to sleep.

***

In the morning, Cadgett and Claudia bathed, dressed and went down for breakfast. Mrs. Penrose was waiting.

"I heard you made a proper fool of yourself in the Quarter Moon last night," she said.

"I probably did," he agreed.

"What happened?" Claudia wanted to know.

"He tried to bribe the bartender into selling him more spirits than he was entitled to, that's what happened. Mr. Trenerry was almost driven to call the constable to take your Yank friend here off to jail. That a guest of mine should behave so shamefully is something I'll have to live down. I'll thank you both if you'll leave my house. Today would be most convenient."

"That's a bit extreme, Mrs. Penrose," Claudia said. "He just had a bit too much to drink, that's all."

"The next coach leaves for Truro at 3 p.m.," she said adamantly.

"That's all right," Cadgett said to Claudia. "Let's leave."

"What are we supposed to do until 3 o'clock?" she wondered.

"We'll take in the sights."

Mrs. Penrose put their refund on the table and left the house.

They went to their bedroom, packed and left, luggage in hand. They stopped at the NAAFI for breakfast and were advised that they could visit the castle built by Henry VIII, or the old Norman church of St. Julian's.

"Which do you prefer?" she asked.

"I'm not interested in that pile of rocks back there," he said.

"All right, let's set out for the church."

"It's no real church unless it's a Baptist church," he joked.

"Well, then, instead of waiting for the coach to Truro, we can take the ferry to Falmouth and get a coach from there. They run more often. We won't have to wait as long."

He agreed. In truth, he had no desire to see the church, either.

Cadgett and Claudia were the only passengers on the small ferry to Prince of Wales pier in Falmouth.

The bus to Plymouth was filled with the usual wartime passengers-civilians going to visit family members in the services and service men and women going to visit their families elsewhere in Britain. They were weary and almost threadbare after more than four years of war. Some carried small packages, gifts no doubt for those they were to meet. They reminded Cadgett of the ubiquitous poor of Kentucky and his heart went out to them.

True, the heavy bombing of cities was past, but the rationing was still strict. What eroded their spirit was not that luxuries were so hard to come by. It was the lack the necessities that made people feel less civilized: a new sweater to replace the one now worn to near disintegration, a pair of shoes with enough heel and sole to permit the wearer to walk without a slight hobble, marmalade for a breakfast that tastes good enough so that a man felt he could do a day's work.

Claudia grew tired watching the countryside pass before her eyes. The bumpy ride on the long-unrepaired road wearied her and she fell asleep on Cadgett's shoulder. He watched her as she slept. Her skin was white, peach, and pink, and smooth as that of a healthy child's. He ran his fingers lightly over her cheek. She stirred but did not wake. Her hair glowed lemon as the late afternoon sun fell on it through the bus's window. He watched her breasts rise and fall in a steady rhythm, then he kissed her lips gently, barely touching them with his. She awoke, looked at him, and, to his delight, smiled.

"Do you think we'll ever be able to repair the damage?" she asked.

"Sure. It was just a misunderstanding."

"Perhaps we can never really blend."

"We don't have to. We just have to love."

"I don't know," she sighed.

"We'll write to each other," Cadgett said emphatically, "We'll be faithful. We'll plan to spend the rest of our lives together. I'm fierce in love with you."

He gazed down at her and enjoyed her eyes as if they were objects of reverence.

"I don't know if that's enough."

"Sure it's enough. It's always been enough."

"Let me think. I have a lot of thinking to do. All I ever wanted was an ordinary English life, to be married to an ordinary man, someone who will know what I think even before I think it. You've upset everything, muddled my mind and set me off into different emotional channels. You've brought uncertainty, tension. My body has revolted against my mind."

"I bring love, too."

"A difficult love."

"Isn't that a more exciting love?"

Cadgett and Claudia left the bus in Plymouth and sat down together in a corner of the terminus where they believed they were less likely to attract notice. Cadgett reached out and took her hand. They sat quietly for several long moments oblivious to the comings and goings around them.

"I have to go," Claudia said. "There's my bus."

"Let's run away together," he suggested. "To Scotland where there's hills. We'll hide until the war ends."

"You wouldn't...."

He was silent for a moment. "No," he said. "I couldn't. I could never do that." He reached out and embraced her. "Goddamn it, why did I let this happen?"

"It just happened," she replied.

"Yes," he agreed and kissed her. "I'll be back as soon as I can. I'll do everything I can to make you happy. I swear it."

"Yes," Claudia answered. "I know that." She broke away, stood up, and walked away, tearfully glancing back at him every ten paces or so.

Chapter XII

Liam thought it would have to be somewhere other than Plymouth. There was too much danger of running into somebody he knew or would meet later on. Southampton sounded more likely. It was a large city, so that the opportunities were there, and was close.

Liam got Bradford's permission to take a three-day furlough, telling him he wanted to visit Catholic churches in Devon. He didn't like to lie, especially to Bradford, but there was no real harm in it.

The trip to Southampton was uneventful. On the train he spoke to no one and no one was interested in speaking to him. The passengers were mostly service men and women, though there was no drinking, no dice playing, no flirting. They all sat in their seats, quietly smoking.

In Southampton he checked into the Star Hotel, bathed, shaved, and gave the chambermaid a half crown to iron his uniform.

It was supper time when he was finally ready. He strolled up the street to the Bar Gate. He came across a small luncheon counter halfway down a side street, and not having eaten since breakfast, ordered a cup of tea and a sandwich.

"Is the weather always this nice in May?" he asked the counter girl.

"Oh, yes," she answered.

He drank the tea and was surprised at how good it tasted. He never drank tea in America where it was barely potable. The difference must be the water, he concluded. The water in England was made for tea, the water in America for coffee.

The girl behind the counter was a pleasant looking teenager with inexperienced brown eyes and a ruddy English complexion. She watched him devour his sandwich.

"Was it good?" she asked.

"It was fine."

She looked genuinely pleased. "More tea?" she asked.

"Yes, thanks."

She poured him another cup and set it down carefully on the counter before him. "Are you one of the Yanks from the park?" she asked.

"The park?"

"Yes, just over the road. The sailors living in the tents."

"No."

He walked the few steps to the entrance and peered up the street. "How long they been there?" he asked her after he returned.

"A fortnight."

"Are they behaving themselves?"

"So far," she giggled.

When she turned around to place a cup and saucer in the sink, he looked her over. She wore a flower print dress that was smooth around her bottom. Her waist was cinched by a black cloth belt and her sturdy legs were stockingless. When she turned back to face him, she smiled.

"Do you live nearby?" he asked, hoping his tone was proper.

"Not terribly far."

"Do you go straight home after work?"

"Not always," she answered.

"When do you get off work?"

"An hour from now."

Liam stirred his tea unnecessarily and took a deep breath. His discomfort reddened his neck and heated

152

his cheeks.

"I'm new here. Don't know anyone. Would you walk with me after you get off work?"

"I'd like that." She smiled candidly.

"I'll have a look around and meet you here in an hour. Is that all right?"

"Yes," she said.

Surprised at how easy it had been, Liam was pleased with himself. He walked a little more confidently than before and sighed with satisfaction.

When he returned to the snack bar after a lonely hour on a park bench, he found the English girl in animated conversation with a British soldier.

"What makes you think I should wait every night for you not knowing whether you'll show up or not?" she snapped at him.

"I'm here now, ain't I?"

"I have other friends, you know."

"Oh, stop the silly stuff and come along."

Liam was embarrassed. He felt as if he had intruded upon a family quarrel.

"Perhaps it's best if I come back later," Liam said.

"Why don't you come back *very* much later," the soldier retorted, "Like *never*."

"You stay right here, Yank," the girl said. "Donald is leaving right now, aren't you, Donald?"

Donald, a short, thin man with a nervous demeanor, exploded with anger.

"A typical Southampton trick," he cried. "A typical Southampton trick. Take the bloody tart," he exclaimed, and he stalked off, his body jerking with anger.

"I'm sorry," Liam told her as he watched the soldier leave. "I didn't mean to cause trouble. Go after him. I'll see you another time."

"Oh, let the fool go. Come on, you promised me a walk."

Liam watched the man until he disappeared around the corner. The girl put her arm in Liam's and they walked to the park.

The setting was similar to American parks

dropped into urban areas to provide some illusion of natural surroundings. Even the one-story brick utility building was familiar to Liam, built on the cheap to contain public lavatories, maintenance equipment and meeting rooms. Only now it housed the mess tables, head and sick bay for American Navy men living in the tents nearby. The Americans, in their dungaree trousers, chambray shirts, and white caps, lolled about in the grass with nothing to do but wait for meals. Some sat on park benches with teenage English girls thrilled to be getting the focused attention the young sailors were giving them. Two English boys batted a cricket ball back and forth, ignoring the few Americans who waited in vain to be invited to try their hand with a cricket bat.

"I forgot to ask you your name," Liam said.

"Dianna," she responded.

Her hair was parted on one side and flowed down to her shoulders where it turned up like a walnut-colored wave. Her eyes were the same color as her hair and her carmine lips were ample and attractive, even alluring.

"You don't act like a Yank," she said as they walked along the paved path leading deeper into the park.

"Really? Why not?"

"You don't give off that randy impatience most of them do."

Liam was impressed. "Randy impatience" was a surprisingly fine phrase coming from a lunch counter girl.

"Oh, but I am," he replied quickly.

"Oh, you're not. Come on now."

"Just wait. Just you wait," he promised. "You'll have to call the cops to restrain me."

"Oh, goodness." She laughed a light, endearing laugh.

Then she said, "This is as far as we can go. The Army takes over from here on. Flack batteries up ahead."

"Is that where your angry friend is from?"

"Yes. Don't mind him. He's jealous of Yanks."

He steered her to a bench and they sat down. "Can't take the competition?"

"More than that. Says he heard a Yank ask where the yellow was in the British flag."

"Funny. I heard the same story, only it was a Brit who said it about the American flag."

"Well, there you have it," she said. "Misunderstanding. Makes for trouble all over." Then she added, "You haven't told me your name,"

"Oh, I'm sorry," he told her. "Davis, David Davis."

"Nice British name, that," she observed.

"You live with your parents?" he asked.

"I do. My dad's with the shipyard."

They sat and chatted about nothing in particular until it began to grow dark.

"My goodness." She looked away from him toward the darkening sky. "I had no idea we've been sitting here that long."

"Do you want me to take you home?" Liam asked.

"Only if you want to."

An air raid siren sounded. Its scream startled him. This was his first experience with an alert ashore.

"What do we do now?" he asked her.

"You're not scared, are you?"

"Sure I am."

"That's because you're not used to it. Come along. We'll go down to the shelter. You'll feel safe there."

She led him to the entrance to an air raid shelter he had passed before but not noticed. Instead of stairs, there was a ramp leading down to a small room with benches along bare concrete walls.

"Where is everybody?" he wondered.

He had expected the nearby residents to have hurried to the shelter by now.

"Home."

"Home? Don't they go to the shelters during a raid?"

"When the Jerries were dropping bombs, they

155

did. Now they just fly over and take pictures."

"Shall we leave, then?"

The moment he finished the sentence he heard the sound of guns.

"I take that back," Liam said.

The gunfire became ear-achingly loud, sounding as if it were coming from just a few yards away. He had not realized how close they were to the guns.

"Wow!" he exclaimed, and covered his ears.

"It won't last long," she shouted over the din.

With remarkable coincidence, the guns ceased firing. Liam and Dianna sat there in the dark listening to the gunfire retreat farther and farther away.

"It's over," she declared, just as the sirens sounded the All Clear.

Liam knew this was the time. The opportunity was there, and might not occur again. He leaned toward her and place his arms on her shoulders. She did not pull back.

He kissed her. Her lips were dry. He felt no emotion, no arousal. He slipped his hand between the buttons down the front of her dress and pulled her brassiere up, freeing one breast. He cupped it in his hand. Her breast was small, globular and warm to the touch.

"Oh, that's nice," she whispered.

He squeezed her breast gently and she began to rock back and forth against the wall of the shelter. He tried to gauge his emotions. Nothing was happening. He was disappointed, but thought perhaps he was being too self-conscious. Yes, that was it. You couldn't become aroused watching yourself. He would stop thinking about it and be spontaneous. He helped her stand up.

"Here," he said, "lie down on the bench."

"No," she replied. "We'll do it standing up. It's safer that way."

"All right."

She took him by the hand to the far side where there were no benches, then she leaned against the wall. In the dark he could just barely make out her movements as he stood there waiting to see what she was going to do. Now she lifted her dress and thrust her pelvis forward. She wore no underwear.

"All right," she whispered. "Now."

He unbuttoning his trousers and lowering them around his knees, he pushed himself against her and felt himself penetrate the curtain of lissome threads.

"Put it in, David."

"Yes."

"What's wrong?" she asked, breathing in short gasps.

"Nothing."

Now he began to thrust against her moist vulva. Time and again he pushed, but he was flaccid, limp.

"Come on, David, what's wrong?"

"I can't," he groaned.

"Try."

"I have been trying. It's no use."

"You're just nervous. Here..." she said, reached down and stroked him with one finger just under and behind the glans. "This will do it."

It didn't. He pulled up his trousers, then buttoned the fly. He turned and began to run from the shelter. Halfway up the ramp he could hear her calling after him.

"Come back. It's all right. It's all right."

Once on the street, he hurried back to the hotel where he lay down on his bed fully clothed until he fell asleep from exhaustion.

When he woke the next morning the shame he felt the night before still lingered, but he knew now what he needed to know. All at once he felt relieved and began to whistle, "Oh, What a Beautiful Morning."

157

Chapter XIII

Something in the Battle Orders that finally arrived aboard the LST *1525* brought Bradford, Fitzpatrick, and Cadgett together for a serious conference -- the line that read: "Attack by enemy aircraft, submarines, and E-boats may be expected en route to and in the exercise area."

"What do you make of it, Commodore?" Cadgett questioned, asking Bradford's opinion for the first time.

Bradford's countenance showed indifference. He lifted his right arm, opened his hand in an unintended gesture of oath taking, his eyes revealed no concern.

"That language is part of the exercise. They're making it as realistic as possible."

Cadgett frowned and pulled at the skin around his Adam's apple.

"Sounds like they want on the record something they didn't want to tell you."

"I don't think so, Captain. The Brits aren't going to approve the sending out of eight precious LSTs and thousands of D-day, troops if they think there's real danger."

Liam at first decided to hold his council. He did not believe he had the experience or rank to take exception. Then the civilian in him emerged and he decided to expose his feelings. He knew if he didn't he would feel like a pusillanimous puppy for days after.

"I think Captain Cadgett has a legitimate concern, sir," he interjected, provoking a surprised look from Cadgett, who never would have expected an ally in Liam. "I heard while ashore that there have been ten ships sunk by E-boats in the area where we are going to hold our exercise."

"That's just it," Bradford agreed. "Those previous actions will have the Brits on the alert more than ever. This convoy is of greater importance than those previous ship movements."

"There is still time until we sail. Plenty of time to get answers about how they intend to protect us," Cadgett insisted.

Bradford pulled his head back and wrinkled his brow. "Captain, I can't question the Royal Navy as if I doubt they know what they're doing."

Cadgett's demeanor suddenly changed. From a reasonable subordinate, he reverted to the adversarial cynic.

"Maybe you don't remember Convoy PQ-17, Commodore, but goddamn it, I do. On their way with supplies for the Russians, the Royal Navy ordered the escorts to scatter starwise when they thought Kraut ships were in the area. Know how many Allied ships went down? How many American ships went down?"

"Yes, I know, Captain, but this situation is quite different."

"In a pig's ass," Cadgett swore. "I'll bet the Germans know all about this exercise already."

"You are quite right to be concerned, Captain. I'll bring it up with the British if I find I can inquire without embarrassing them."

Cadgett scowled, turned on his heels and walked from the cabin muttering under his breath.

**

The Royal Navy could spare only two escort vessels to accompany the eight LSTs of convoy M-6 to Strangull Strand for Exercise Mongoose.

HMS *Espadon*, a dottering World War I destroyer, was anchored in Plymouth harbor ready to get underway to join with the corvette *HMS Marigold* to protect convoy M-6.

In the *Espadon's* wardroom, the captain of the sluggish old vessel offered his second in command, his Number One, a cup of tea and almost casually informed him of their upcoming assignment.

"The *Marigold* will be joining us for this exercise," he said.

"Strangull Strand again?" Number One asked.

"Yes," the captain acknowledged, plainly bored with the prospect. He gulped his tepid tea and crouched over the wardroom table, his elbows supporting him.

"Flotilla of Yank LSTs. You know the drill. They unload on the beach. We wait till the soldiers finish their playing, then reload. We stand to off shore watching for Jerry."

"Then back to Plymouth and do it all over again," Number One sighed.

Abandoning their nearly empty tea cups on the table, they went up to the navigation bridge.

"Nice night for April," the captain observed.

"We'll have filthy weather tomorrow to make up for it, rest assured."

"No doubt."

"What the devil!" Number One suddenly cried.

"What is it Derek?" the captain asked, casting his eyes around.

"That LCT is drifting right toward us."

"Christ!" the captain exclaimed, then shouted, "Stand by for collision!"

The shovel-nosed tank landing craft had slipped its mooring and gone adrift in Plymouth harbor. It was stopped only at the barrier presented by HMS *Espadon.*

A sudden crushing, then a scraping noise startled the crew below decks and sent them dashing topside, while the aged ship jarred backwards and trembled. The LCT recoiled from the collision, then disengaged itself from the *Espadon* and drifted off.

"Oh, no, dammit!" the captain cried, grinding his

teeth and slamming his right fist into the open palm of his other hand. "Number One, report the collision then have the engineer let me know how much damage we've sustained."

"Aye, sir," Number One said, had the collision reported, then called the Engineering Officer over the voice tube.

It did not take long to assess the damage. It was visible from both outside and in.

"Well, what's the bad news, Harry?" the Captain asked.

"Damage slight. Small hole and distorted plating."

"Can you fix?"

"Yes."

"No danger of shipping water?"

"No, sir."

"Even in heavy seas?"

"Don't think so, sir."

"So we can proceed with our orders?"

"Unfortunately, yes, sir."

The captain laughed. His stomach, which had now just begun to bulge from the years and ale, shook. He placed his hand over his pulsating abdomen and held his flesh still.

"I know what you mean, Harry, but go we must."

"Aye, sir," Harry answered.

The captain then ordered the signalman to report to him.

"Message the port commander: "At 4:45 a.m. whilst laying stopped as marker vessel rammed by American landing craft. Damage plating distorted and holed at forecastle 22 station 2 feet above waterline. Advise. Cpt. R. Thomas, Commanding, HMS *Espadon*."

After an hour's wait for a reply it came blinking from the port commander's signal light: "What is your assignment?"

The captain ordered the reply: "Escort landing exercise."

The answer: "Stay behind for repairs."

The captain looked up from the signalman's

scribbled recording of the message and repressed a smile. This meant several days in port. Perhaps a week. He could hardly contain himself.

"Good news, fellows," the captain said, "We've been reprieved."

CHAPTER XIV

Kommodore Gunther Friedrich, a tall, bald, German naval officer, leaned against the wall of his Cherbourg headquarters and pointed to a large chart of the English Channel. "Paul," he called out, "Paul, you're not dozing are you?"

Kapitanleutnant Paul Gass lifted his head from the table and smiled grimly. "Me, dozing? Ridiculous, Gunther. After all, I've had at least four hours sleep the last two days. Keeping those boats in condition has been, as the Tommies say, 'a piece of cake'."

"I know it's difficult, but we're up against it now, my friend. They're coming any day now. How many boats are fit for sea?"

"Six. But it's not so much the boats as the men. They're tired. No leave. Awake nights with the bombing."

"We can comfort ourselves knowing that if the landings are repelled, we can all take a rest. It will be a long time until the English and the Amis recover. Here, let's dispense with the chart. We know it by heart anyway. Let's talk over a cup of coffee."

Friedreich stepped away from the wall and slid into a seat at the table next to Gass.

"Krebbs!" he shouted, "Krebbs!"

The door swung open and an elderly orderly appeared.

"Yes, sir!"

"Krebbs, get the *Kapitanleutnant* and me some coffee, and you might as well include a couple of croissants."

"Yes, sir," he said and marched away quietly, carefully closing the door behind him.

"Is it going to be blind or do we know something?" Gass inquired.

"We know something," Friedrich answered. *B-Dienst* tells us there's been a sudden increase in radio traffic around Lyme Bay. We should go out and have a look."

There was a polite knock on the door.

"Come in, Krebbs," Friedrich shouted.

Krebbs pushed the door open with the tray he held in his hands. He walked to the table and laid it before the two naval officers.

"Thank you, Krebbs," Friedrich said. "Make sure the door is closed behind you."

"Yes, sir," Krebbs replied and left.

Gass, a youthful looking 30-year-old with dark brown hair, a gaunt face, and a ski jump nose that made him look more Slavic than German, sipped some coffee, picked up a croissant and stared at it.

"Delicious, aren't they? The food, the wine, the women. Here in France, if it weren't for the bombing..."

"Even back home the food situation is certainly better than the First World War," Friedrich said, taking a cup of coffee for himself.

"I wouldn't know," Gass countered. "I do know that the French women are marvelous."

Friedrich's sense of humor was irrepressible. He would often remonstrate with himself after joking with men of lower rank, wondering if he was undermining discipline.

"Women, Gass, are an occupied nation's most valuable natural resource."

"How?" said Gass, feigned naiveté.

"It's a natural resource that doesn't need cultivating, mining, or manufacturing. It doesn't wear out or get used up."

"The vaginal theory of economics," Gass joked.

Gass buttered his croissant carefully, leaving no part of the roll uncovered, then inspected his work, bit into it and chewed with a grinding movement of his narrow jaw.

"Shove off at 0200 hours, Paul," Friedreich remarked off- handedly. Shunning dramatics when he gave combat orders, he tried to make them sound routine. He knew that men who have experienced combat resent the dramatic as much as they do the sentimental.

Gass did not answer. Instead, he got up, gave a relaxed salute and left, unfinished croissant in hand, to alert his crews.

***

Six German E-boats, each with two torpedoes in their tubes ready to fire, a 40mm gun on their forward deck and a newly installed 37mm gun aft, followed Gass's boat out of Cherbourg harbor into the choppy English Channel.

"Here we go again," Gass declared wiping the spindrift from his face. "Let's wish ourselves luck."

"Luck!" *Lieutenant* Sieber clapped his skipper on the back.

***

The *1525* with four sister ships in a column behind it, sailed from Plymouth harbor to rendezvous with the other three ships of the flotilla.

The tank decks of the LSTs were crowded with tanks, DUKW amphibious vehicles, jeeps and trucks of every type. The army crews stayed near their vehicles or slept in the cabs. The same situation prevailed on the open main deck, which also was jammed with vehicles and their crews. The men assigned to be transported in them lolled nearby.

In the port and starboard troop compartments on both sides of the tank deck, soldiers, along with their personal arms and equipment, were packed in close enough to smell one another's breath.

The column of five LSTs had barely cleared the harbor's submarine barrier when some of the GIs were sick. They lay moaning on the decks, in their bunks, and hung over the ship's rail vomiting. The sailors had forgotten their early days of sea sickness and looked upon the GIs with disgust. The crewmen considered themselves "old salts" now and had acquired the age-old sailor's contempt for landlubbers.

The evening was pleasant, brisk, but not cold enough to drive Cadgett to take shelter in the wheelhouse. After a while Bradford came up to the conn and positioned himself near Cadgett. Cadgett ignored him and stood by as the pilot they picked up before sailing gave the orders.

"Chilly," Bradford commented to Cadgett as they stood on the open conn together.

Bradford's attempt at small talk failed to engage Cadgett, who grunted and moved a step farther away from him.

There were times Cadgett could hardly tolerate being in Bradford's presence and had been heard to mutter, "There's not enough room on this bridge for both of us." He moved to the extreme end of the conn, standing as far from the commodore as he could. He glanced at him. What was he, five foot six...seven? A runt. Cadgett had noticed Bradford's stomach protruding almost imperceptibly behind his belt, the beginning of a jar-head gunny sergeant's beer belly. Yet he stands there with all the confidence in the world, he thought, like he designed, built and floated this ship. He thinks he shits strawberry ice cream. And that candy-assed aide of his. He's just waiting for me to make a mistake so he can say to his asshole buddies, "He's just a shit-kicking hillbilly." Well, like they say back in Turkey Hollow: "Fuck 'em all but six and save them for pallbearers."

The arrival on the bridge of Liam prompted a smile of greeting from the commodore and a scowl from Cadgett. Liam handed a just-decoded message to Bradford, who read it without comment.

Unable to restrain his curiosity, Cadgett reluctantly asked about the message.

"Anything important, Commodore?"

"No, Captain."

Cadgett was annoyed that Bradford did not reveal the contents of the message to him but resisted pressing him.

A newcomer appeared on the bridge and took a place near Cadgett. He was a tall, undistinguished looking man in his early thirties, with a severe haircut and the scattered scars of a formerly carbuncular complexion. He wore grays rather than khakis, though he did not appear to be concerned about his different color uniform or intimidated by the higher ranks of the two men he joined.

"My new executive officer. Name is Long," introduced Cadgett."Long, this is Commodore Bradford. And that there is Mr. Fitzpatrick, who shouldn't be up here now that he's delivered the message."

Long saluted Bradford and shook hands with Fitzpatrick, who quickly left the bridge and headed below.

The remaining men stood on the conn pulling up their cold weather jackets to shelter their necks.

"The pilot's drunk," Lieutenant Long informed them.

Cadgett turned to observe the pilot's behavior. He was acting a bit tipsy, but the orders he gave the helmsman and the engine room guided the ship in what seemed to Cadgett an unerring path. Cadgett shrugged and returned to watching the harbor channel ahead.

"Isn't that our escort, the *Marigold*, coming our way?" Long remarked.

Cadgett turned his attention to an approaching British corvette. "Looks like her," Cadgett said.

"Wait until she passes abeam of us. We'll check her out," Bradford suggested.

"By Christ, she is our escort," Cadgett said as she passed. He turned to Bradford."Okay, Commodore, what the hell's going on?"

Bradford glanced at the escort, then back at

Cadgett. "I suspect she's going to take a position at the end of the column."

"Our other escort is supposed to be Tail End Charlie. Don't tell me this a new tactic. Two at the tail of the column, none at the head."

"I don't know, Captain, but I am sure there's a good reason for whatever is happening."

"I think the Brits are as fucked up as a two-car nigra funeral," Cadgett spat.

Bradford said, "They've been at this a while. Give them credit for having some knowledge of how to conduct a convoy."

"I hope your confidence in the Brits is well placed, Commodore, or we're going to find ourselves in deep shit."

"Yes, Captain, I'm sure we will if they're as confused as your image conveys."

Lieutenant Long tittered. "Going to the head," he mumbled and still laughing, retreated to the chartroom.

After dropping the pilot, who misjudged a rung and nearly fell off the Jacob's ladder, Cadgett took over and guided his ship into the open waters of the English Channel.

To their surprise they saw the HMS *Marigold* passing them to starboard.

Long, having now brought himself under control, returned from the chartroom and took his former place.

"You see." Bradford smiled in triumph. "They've exchanged places. The *Marigold* is now moving to the head of the column."

Lieutenant Long raised his binoculars to his eyes and looked searchingly astern. He then addressed Cadgett directly, ignoring Bradford. "I don't see the other escort at the end of the column," he reported.

"Well, what do you say now, Commodore?" Cadgett questioned angrily.

"I have no doubt the missing escort will soon make its presence known," Bradford stated.

"Let us pray," Cadgett said.

"An excellent suggestion, Captain," Bradford said. "Don't you agree, Mr. Long?"

"Yes, sir. Never does any harm."

They stood in silence for a time until they spied three ships approaching at a slow speed.

"There they are," Bradford noted when he caught sight of the ships that made up the rest of the flotilla. "Right on time."

"Should I signal them to fall in behind us?" Cadgett asked Bradford without looking at him.

"No need," Bradford replied. "They have their orders."

Through the darkness, the men watched the three lumbering LSTs, loaded with soldiers, equipment, and vehicles, come into line behind the last ship in the column. Bradford ordered Cadgett to make a wide, looping turn.

Cadgett related the order to the OOD, then asked, "What's that turn about, Commodore? I wish you would have briefed me back in Plymouth. Every move comes as a surprise."

"I tell you what you need to know when you need to know it," Bradford said. "It's best that way."

Glumly, Cadgett accepted Bradford's pronouncement.

"Slow to four knots, Captain."

"What the hell's going on? Would you fill me in, sir?"

"We're simulating the time it would take us to make the cross-Channel sailing," Bradford told him.

"Thanks," Cadgett replied grudgingly.

"Sir, I still see only one of the two escorts listed in the Battle Orders," Long broke in, "that British corvette at the head of the column."

"Captain Cadgett and I have already discussed that, Mr. Long. Don't trouble yourself about it. The other escort will be along soon."

Cadgett said nothing but moved as far from Bradford as he could get. He peered aft, hiding a concerned look.

***

"Looks as if our old friends are back, Captain," Lieutenant Reeves, First Lieutenant of the destroyer HMS *Winslow*, said. "Message says, ships on port wave."

The captain immediately gave the order to proceed at full speed toward Lyme Bay. The "ships" were either E-boats or surfaced U-boats. He guessed E-boats. It would be startling indeed if U-boats were present in a pack in the English channel and on the surface, to boot.

A half hour later he heard Reeves shout up to him, "Blips on the radar, sir!"

"What do you make of them, Number One?"

"Almost certainly E-boats, Captain."

Captain Adams was not rattled by the report. He had faced E-boats before. Dangerous foes they were, but the crews of British warships sailing the Channel felt as safe as anywhere at sea. There were always other British ships nearby to call on for help, and there were coastal guns should the Jerries be reckless enough to sail close to shore.

"Let's try to run them down," Captain Adams decided, feeling his blood rise as it always did at the start of a sea hunt. He knew it would probably come to nothing. The British chasing, the Germans fleeing. How he would love to catch the bastards! Yes, the Jerries would go after a destroyer if they could sneak up on it unaware. If not, they more often would retire than attack. That, after all, was only prudent.

"Ahead full!" the captain ordered and the ship responded with a thrust of engine power, creating a turbulent wake as she smashed into a wall of placid waters.

"Radio that there are E-boats on the hunt in the Lyme Bay area," the captain ordered. "There's a Yank convoy out there with eight thousand soldiers aboard."

"Immediately, sir." With that Reeves hurried to the radio operator to send the message out on the emergency frequency.

***

Chasing 30-knot motor torpedo boats in his slower vessel, Captain Adams was not surprised to hear Lieutenant Reeves say, "They're widening their lead, sir."

"Any chance at all of us catching them?"

"Not really, sir."

"Very well, let's keep after them for a little while longer in case the gods are good to us and one of them breaks down. Meanwhile, see if you can light them up with flares. I want to send a few shots their way. Maybe it will deflect them from their destination."

The flares arced in the night sky above and burst into a yellow light that revealed a few barely visible blobs on the horizon. The futile shots that followed threw up geysers of water short and wide of the targets.

***

"Flares, sir," Lieutenant Long, the new executive officer pointed out.

"Where?" Cadgett asked.

"There, sir." He stretched out his arm to indicate in the direction of the short-lived light he had caught from the corner of his eye.

"A long way off," Bradford observed.

The shock of the sudden sound of distant gunfire silenced them for a few moments.

"Oh, oh," Lieutenant Long said.

"Coxswain, get down below and tell Mr. Fitzpatrick he's wanted on the bridge," Bradford ordered, then glanced at Cadgett who shrugged resignedly.

"Something's going on in the Channel," Long said.

Cadgett lifted his chin and placed his hands on his

171

hips. He was suddenly in deep thought, evaluating the flares, the gunfire, the distance and his own position. He was imagining a series of scenarios, seeking the most logical.

Liam appeared, trying to rub the tiredness from his eyes with his knuckle.

"Let's get to the radio shack and see if something's coming in," Cadgett advised. "You, too, Mr. Fitzpatrick. We'll need a decoder."

***

"What's the radar tell us about our pursuers, Sieber?" Gass wanted to know, his eyes trying to penetrate the darkness to the point at which he calculated the sky and sea met.

"They're so far back they're off the screen," Sieber replied.

"And the convoy?"

"Up ahead. We're closing on them."

"All right, then. When we're in position we'll fire first. I'll tell you when to send up the signal flare for the rest of the boats to cut loose."

Now the night enveloped them and the certainty of imminent combat with the enemy had their hearts pounding. Peering into the dark, hands perspired and jaws tightened. Suddenly, a weak moon emerged from behind ragged black clouds and they could make out the shapes of a column of eight ships ahead.

"Derner, hard left," Gass ordered. "I want to come at them from leeward. We'll be less expected coming in from the coast."

Gass licked his desiccated lips and could hardly restrain his excitement. There was no evidence that his boats were observed.

"All right. Let's light them up for the other boats.

Without taking the time to acknowledge the order to fire, Sieber passed it on. The bam, bam, bam of the 40mm started immediately. A few moments passed before the tracer rounds ignited. The German ammunition would give no clue to the enemy of where the firing originated.

"Swing wide to starboard, Derner," the captain yelled over the pulsing roar of the engines and the sound of the plowed sea.

He waited as long as he could contain himself, then began shouting further orders.

"Slow to ten knots. Nice! Fine! Good! A little to port! I want to take the one at the end of the column. Good! Steady as she goes. All right, fire one and two!"

Aboard the LST *2631* some of the crew heard a strange scraping sound. Unknown to them, one of the torpedoes grazed the hull of the ship as it passed beneath. None of them commented on the reverberations. One hears noises aboard a ship at sea that nobody can explain.

The Germans watched their torpedoes splash into the Channel and almost immediately lost track of them as they sped through black waters toward the LST *2631*.

Gass waited for the crack of the torpedoes hitting. The minutes passed with agonizing slowness, until at last he had to recognize with almost paralyzing disappointment that the shots had missed.

"Goddamn it!" Gass blasphemed, then cursed himself for being too impatient to close further before he fired his torpedoes. He would not repeat the mistake. "Order the boats not to fire until they've closed to 3,000 meters. Then pick out their targets and go to it."

"Aye, sir." Sieber said, then instructed the signalman on the color of the flares to be sent up.

***

Afterwards nobody could say exactly where the torpedo struck the *2631*. Lieutenant Ernest Bergstrom was on his way topside from the wardroom when a powerful explosion hurled him into the air. When he landed back on the deck, he was covered with dust and loosend rust. His legs ached and streams of blood ran down his calves. His head pained him and he was deaf from the ear-crushing blast. Under his feet the deck had buckled and it took him several long moments to reorient himself.

After pulling himself together, Bergstrom hobbled down the passageway to find someone who could tell him what had happened. As he approached the hatch leading to the tank deck, he heard roaring sounds and the screams of men in unbearable agony. Alarmed, he swung open the hatch. There he saw that the fuel tanks of vehicles jammed one behind the other on the tank deck had exploded, spraying fire on the soldiers who stood on the deck next to their jeeps, tanks, and trucks. Men broiled like dinner meat, flamed like torches and screamed like butchered animals.

A barrier of flames suddenly blasted up between Bergstrom and the screaming men. Then, in obedience to standing orders, he closed the watertight hatch and secured it with a dogging bar. No man on the tank deck could now escape death, but the rest of the ship would for a time be isolated from the fire.

Half sick from what he had done, Bergstrom stumbled up to the deck to a scene of utter horror. Soldiers and sailors milled around waiting to be told what to do. Others took their fate into their own hands and leaped into the sea. Some soldiers drowned immediately, pulled under by the heavy equipment they were wearing. Others died because they neglected to remove their helmets before they jumped, their necks broken from the snap-back of the helmet strap when they hit the water. Many died because nobody had thought to teach them how to use the CO_2 inflated lifebelts they had been issued. The lifebelts were designed to be pulled up around the neck to support the wearer's head above water. The men assumed the belts were meant to be kept around their waists. With their belts around their waists their heads were plunged into the sea and they drowned.

Some soldiers and a few sailors refused to jump into the icy Channel waters. Some protested that they didn't know how to swim; others were paralyzed by the sight of the long drop into waters now aflame with burning fuel oil.

Bergstrom approached one man he knew and urged him to jump.

"No," the man said, "I can't swim."

"I'll jump with you," Bergstrom told him.

"Promise you won't leave me?"

"I promise."

They climbed over the ship's rail and, holding each other around the waist, leaped into the sea. As soon as they hit the water, the man grabbed Bergstrom around the shoulders and held on with a strength that can come only from terror. Bergstrom tried to free himself, all the time assuring the bug-eyed man he could save them both if he released him. In response, the man only tightened his grip. Bergstrom lifted himself from the water just enough to let loose with a powerful punch to the side of the man's head. The man let go and Bergstrom swam away. When he looked back, the man was nowhere to be seen. Bergstrom swam toward a life raft he could make out in the light of his burning ship. When he got there, he found there was no more room aboard. He then joined with the other late arrivals in trying to stay afloat.

***

Coxswain Ken Bloch was in his bunk when the torpedo hit. The force of the explosion raised him high enough for his head to strike the overhead. He assumed there'd been an accident. He jumped out of his bunk and headed topside, his head aching.

On deck, he immediately knew his assumption was wrong. Now he knew they'd been hit by a torpedo. He saw a man jump into the sea and go straight down without coming back up and he wondered why. Surely the man could have bobbed to the surface. Could someone be so disoriented that he commits suicide? Evidently, more than one were. Later, he again observed the same puzzling phenome-

175

non.

Bloch raced for a place on the deck where he knew there was a raft. When he got there he found a mob of men trying to free it from the cables that secured it to its place. The soldiers and crewmen trying to get the raft overboard found that the cables were frozen to the frame by rust and brine.

"Give me that rifle," a naval officer yelled at a GI standing nearby. "I'm going to shoot the fucker loose."

"Here," the soldier said, "but don't forget who gave you the rifle. Save me a spot on the raft."

"Goddamn you," the officer cried and tore the M1 from his hands. The officer raised the weapon and fired at the cable. It took a few shots, but the wire parted and the men around the raft manhandled it overboard.

Bloch realized there would be no room for him on that raft. He began to look for another. The deck under his bare feet grew hot from the fire below. Bloch ran to the rail, climbed over it, and jumped into the gelid waters of the Channel.

Treading water, he watched the *2631* flounder. She now lay partially submerged below the surface. Bloch swam to his ship's protruding bow and grabbed hold. He would hang on there, his body immersed in the numbing water, for hours.

***

Motor Machinist Mate Dominick De Laura was in the *2631*'s engine room when the torpedo struck.

"What happened?" De Laura asked a nearby shipmate when he heard the explosion.

"Beats the shit out of me," the other motor mac said and took off for the ladder.

"Let's get out of here!" another cried and they all headed for the ladders.

When De Laura arrived on deck, he was stunned by the mad scene. Men were running every which way while others leaped overboard. Some were just sitting on the deck waiting for God knows what. He was shocked to see men he knew lying on the deck dead or severely wounded. He suddenly got the idea to climb up to the navigation bridge and get to one of the LCVPs.

He knew the 36-foot landing boats doubled as lifeboats and carried survival equipment. De Laura climbed up the ladder to the bridge only to discover that he was not the only one to have thought of getting to the boats.

A naval officer, who had never before lowered an LCVP, tried to get its mechanism to work and failed. The boat had been damaged by the explosion of the torpedo and it was stuck, hanging bow up from the davits, swinging to and fro.

The officer finally gave up, turned around and confronted the just-arrived De Laura.

"Get me an ax, sailor!" he ordered.

De Laura hurried into the superstructure where he remembered an ax hung on the bulkhead. He grabbed it, ran back to the boat and handed it to the officer who began to chop away at the cables. The man finally managed to cut through, and the boat fell into the sea, overturned, floundered, and sank. Men groaned in disappointment as they made their way down to the main deck to jump into the water and an uncertain fate.

Now the waters around the blazing *2631* were dotted with bobbing heads.

***

Lieutenant Bill Clark was one of the last to jump overboard from the *2631*. He had expended much precious time begging and cajoling soldiers to strip off their equipment and jump into the Channel. Oddly, some did not want to discard their packs and rifles and as a result drowned in seconds. Others heeded Clark's advice and drowned anyway.

He finally gave up on the remaining few soldiers who refused to listen to him and jumped into the sea himself. Treading water, he looked around to decide what to do. Spying a raft some distance from him, he swam toward it. When he got there he found it over-loaded with men. He grabbed the loop of rope that was hanging from the raft for just that purpose. Next to him was a man whose head and face were covered with blood. He was whimpering, ready to give up.

"That's enough," the man said. "I'm letting go."

"Wait!" Clark implored him. "Let me get you aboard the raft."

"I tried," the man said, "but they won't give me a spot."

"The hell you say," Clark declared, and pulled his head high enough out of the water to see the executive officer of the ship sitting in the middle of the raft, shivering.

"Hey, Mr. Petz. I have a wounded man here who needs to get out of the water."

"This is my spot," Lieutenant Petz answered.

"All right," Clark told him. "I'm going to count to three. If your ass isn't in the water by then I'm going to pull you in and hold your head under until you're a dead man. One...two...th...."

At that, Petz slipped into the sea and grabbed hold of an attached loop of rope.

Clark helped the wounded man onto the raft with the aid of two men already aboard.

"Thanks, Mr. Clark," the wounded sailor said.

"Think nothing of it," Clark answered jauntily. "Next time we're on a sinking ship you can help me get on a raft."

The man died soon after and Clark took his place, leaving Lieutenant Petz in the water.

One hour later, there was still no sight of rescuers. A half hour after that, men began to let go of the rope loops and slip beneath the surface. Men died and sank below, or, near death, gave up and drowned.

***

In the crew's quarters on the *1525*, Wheels climbed out of his bunk, got into his dungaree trousers, put on his chambray shirt and foul-weather jacket, pulled on his socks and then his shoes. He topped his shipboard outfit with a blue woolen watch cap. He did not bother to wash. That would have to wait until he was relieved from his station at 0400. He hurried up to the wheelhouse. Like all sailors he feared being late to relieve the quartermaster on duty. Tardiness was one of the most heinous sins a Navy man could commit.

Arriving in the wheelhouse, he silently exchanged places with the quartermaster striker. Within a few minutes, the entire watch had been relieved; there was a new shift on the bridge. Ensign Cornell and three enlisted men replaced their counterparts and took up their duties. Cadgett, Bradford, and Liam were still in the radio shack waiting for a message that would explain what they had seen in the Channel. Wheels noted that the sea was impenetrably dark, the weather clearing, and the weak moon setting.

His hands on the helm and his eyes staring straight ahead, Wheels was the first to see the explosion when the torpedo struck the *2631*. He felt a slight bump and saw a flicker of light from the blast reflect on the sea.

"Something's happened, Mr. Cornell," he called out to the Officer of the Deck.

Ensign Cornell hurried to the starboard port and looked out at the black sea.

"I don't see anything, Wheels."

"I saw a reflection of flames, sir."

"Okay, I'm not going to take the chance of getting my ass eaten out by the skipper. Sound General Quarters."

Wheels let go of the helm just long enough to shout over the P.A. system.

"General Quarters. General Quarters. All hands, man your battle stations. This is not a drill. This is not a drill."

By the time Cadgett, Bradford, and Liam reached the bridge, the flames from the *2631* had begun to illuminate the sky behind them.

"That's not one of our LSTs," Bradford guessed. "It's too far astern."

179

"It could be Tail End Charlie." Liam countered.

"By Christ, I think it is ours," Cadgett cried.

"You think so?" Bradford said. "You think so, Liam?"

"Goddamn it," Cadgett snarled, driving a fist into his palm. "A submarine. This close to England. Jesus! If it were daylight, I could see the coast."

"Hear that?" Liam said huskily.

They all ceased speaking.

"Engines," Bradford broke out. "E-boats!" Liam shouted.

"Oh, no," Bradford exclaimed as the *1525* shuddered from a nearby explosion.

"It's the *2244*. She's been hit," Cadgett said coolly. "Mr. Cornell, go back to the radio shack and ask Sparks if there's anything coming in."

Another explosion and the *1525* shook as if it too had taken a torpedo, but the victim was the *2788*, the third ship in the flotilla to be struck.

Cornell returned with the news.

"Nothing, Captain. Nothing on the frequency we were told to monitor."

"That's great! That's just great! E-boats leave France, slip past the British destroyers, cross the Channel undetected, attack us a few miles off the English coast and the Brits have seen nothing! Heard nothing! Not a fucking thing!"

"Engines again!" Bradford called.

"I can see something," Fitzpatrick added. "Torpedo boats. They're zig zagging in and out of our column."

"Tell Mr. Williams to commence firing just as soon as he sees the bastards." A moment after Cadgett said that, the banging of guns could be heard in the wheelhouse.

"Those are our guns," Bradford cried. "Williams must see them."

"Good. Pepper their asses!" Cadgett shouted as if Williams could hear him.

"Our tracers are hitting the *2446*, Captain," Liam screamed.

"What the hell's the *2446* doing there?" Cadgett

demanded.

"It's swung out of the column," Liam said.

Bradford put his hands to his forehead, squinted his eyes and seemed about to cry. "Message the flotilla to break convoy and immediately head for an English port. They are to stop for nothing!"

The officer of the deck started to leave, carrying our Bradford's order.

"Just a goddamn minute, Mr. Cornell," Cadgett growled. "Where do you think you're going?"

"Back to the radio shack, sir."

Cadgett glared at him threateningly. He held up one finger. "A, I am captain of this ship." He held up two fingers. "B, you are a member of my crew." He held up a third. "C, you take orders from me and only me. Do you understand that, Mr. Cornell? Say! Do you understand that? Well, say, you half-assed excuse for a naval officer. Say!"

Cornell's face crumpled under the insults. Nothing emerged from him but a squeaking sound. Finally words stumbled from his pale lips. "Ye,ye,ye, yes, sir. Yes, sir. I understand, sir."

Cadgett spun around to face Bradford. His eyes were reservoirs of liquid anger. "You want to haul ass?" he shouted, his head jerking with agitation.

"Correct, Captain. I want to *haul ass*. You will do it now." A tiny tic began to pulsate near the corner of Bradford's mouth.

"There are live men in the water, Commodore." Cadgett protested.

Bradford did not directly answer Cadgett. Instead he raised his head challengingly, "Flank speed for Dartmouth, Captain!"

"You're prepared to abandon those men to die?"

"Flank speed for Dartmouth, Captain," he repeated.

"Commodore, I've rolled over, caved, in and backed down for you. But not this time. I'll be goddamned if I'll sail to Dartmouth, to Falmouth, to Exmouth, or any other fucking mouth. There are men dying out there and we can save them."

"Flank speed for Dartmouth, Captain, or you'll

181

face a court martial for disobeying orders under fire."

"No, Commodore!" Cadgett shouted. "Helmsman, come about!"

"I ask you one final time, Captain," Bradford insisted. "Weigh the consequences of a refusal. I order you to make for Dartmouth without stopping."

Cadgett leaped forward as if to strike Bradford. "Commodore," he snarled, glaring at him. "You are responsible only for the flotilla as a whole. Look around you, Commodore. Two ships have been sunk. One ship has had its stern blasted off and the other four are nowhere to be seen. There is no longer a flotilla for you to command. Just this ship for *me* to command. And I command that this ship return to pick up survivors."

"What say you, Mr. Fitzpatrick?" Bradford asked.

"I'm sorry, sir," Liam responded, "we should go back."

"Let's leave it to the crew," Cadgett said with a disingenuous smile. He grabbed the P.A. microphone and spoke into it.

"This is the captain speaking."

The entire ship suddenly froze.

"The Krauts have torpedoed three of our ships. Men are in the water. We can take off like a yella dog or we can go back to save as many as possible, even if it means tangling assholes with the Krauts. We don't stand a chance of a snowball in hell if they're still around but at least we'll go down fighting. What do you say?"

In response, a great shouting went up from every part of the ship. The men reacted with near hysteria. They kicked the bulkheads, slammed their fists against the 20mm gun shields, reached out as if to strangle the specter of a German floating before them. They growled like infuriated animals, snarled like predators and hissed hatred.

"Go back!"

"Tear them to pieces!"

"Let's kill the fuckin' Krauts."

"Fight!"

182

Cadgett grabbed the helmsman by the shoulder, tore him off the wheel and tossed him aside.

"Take the wheel, Mr. Cornell!" he ordered.

Cornell leaped to the helm and grasped it with both hands.

"Now, come about!"

"Aye aye, sir," Cornell said.

"You're sailing into dangerous waters, Captain," Bradford warned.

"That's where regulars like you and me should be, isn't that so, Commodore?"

***

It was almost 0630 when the LST *1525* arrived back at the site of the torpedoings. Bodies bobbed in the sea, lapped by whitecaps that crested on the dark waves. Other men, burned to amorphous lumps, floated like misshapen buoys. Debris was everywhere: empty rafts, half sunken LCVPs, white sailor caps. Smoke rose from submerged parts of vehicles and other detritus of battle. Patches of diesel oil burned on the surface of the sea.

The *1525*'s coxswain, in response to habit, entered the charthouse at exactly 0630 and put the prescribed record on the player. The strains of "Oh, What a Beautiful Morning" swelled out and over the surface of a defiled sea.

Cadgett stormed into the chartroom, spun the hapless boy around, thrust his palm against his chin and with a powerful shove sent him crashing against the bulkhead. The boy slumped to the deck, too astonished even to cry out. He lay there staring with trepidation at his furious skipper.

"Now you get your ass below!" Cadgett said.

"No, sir. I'm staying up here to fight."

Cadgett paused, then let the anger vent from him in a deep exhale. "Good boy," he said and returned to the wheelhouse.

Watching the desolate scene before them, neither Cadgett, Bradford nor Liam said anything.

Bradford rubbed the tears in his eyes with the

knuckles of his right hand. Liam placed his palm over his mouth and forgot to remove it. Cadgett stroked his throat, then picked up the microphone.

"This is the Captain speaking. Boat crews man your boats. Pick up anyone who even seems alive. Leave the dead. Mr. Graves, get a party of men down to the bow doors. Mr. Mullen, open bow doors. We will haul survivors in from the ramp."

He then had both of the ship's LCVPs lowered into the water and ordered their coxswains to get underway.

LCVPs managed to rescue about one hundred survivors and ferry them to the ship's ramp where the pharmicist's mates and a detail of crewmen took them aboard.

"Got them all, McCann?" the Captain shouted down to the young coxswain of one of the boats.

"Yes, sir," he replied.

"How about you?" he asked the coxswain of the other boat.

"Nothing but dead left, sir."

"Okay," Cadgett said. "Let's hoist those boats aboard and head for port."

Cadgett then ordered the ship to sail for Plymouth. Dartmouth was closer but he rejected it because it was the port of refuge Bradford had chosen.

***

The destroyer HMS *Winslow* came upon the scene of devastation just after the *1525* had left for Plymouth.

"Lookout reports debris in the water, sir," the Number One, Lieutenant Reeves, told the captain.

Captain Adams moved to the edge of the bridge and stared down at the flotsam. "Looks fresh," he said.

"It does, sir," Reeves replied.

"Have we been informed about a sinking?"

"No, Captain."

"Let's have a look about."

The captain ordered the engine to slow. The ship

moved almost gently through the water while on the weather decks men stared at the wreckage afloat on the surface of the Channel.

"There's been some unpleasantness here," the captain noted with repressed emotion.

"It was Yanks, sir. Those white caps they wear are all about."

"Poor buggers. Those E-boats, I suppose."

"Captain," said Number One, "The stern lookouts report blood in the water."

"Good God!" the Captain said.

"We're mincing Yanks, sir."

"There's a ship's bow protruding from the water, Number One."

"I see it, sir."

The captain shouted into the voice tube,

"All ahead full."

The ship quickly picked up speed. Within shouting distance of the *2631*'s prow, the Captain ordered the ship to hove to.

"All engines stop," ordered Captain Adams.

"Someone's clinging to the bow," Reeves said.

A dinghy was hastily lowered. The boat crew rowed to the protruding prow as quickly as they could.

"Ahoy! Yank!"

"Come and get me," Bloch said.

"Coming."

Carefully they, eased the boat athwart the *2631*'s bow, and Bloch fell into waiting arms of two British sailors.

On the way back to the *Winslow*, the boat commander questioned the American.

"What ship, Yank?"

"LST *2631*."

"Anyone else alive that you know of?"

"No. I saw a ship from my flotilla pick up some men, but they missed me."

"All right, relax. We'll get you some rum and dry clothes as soon as we get back aboard."

The captain watched the boat's progress from the

bridge. "Only one man," he muttered sadly. "Reeves, report this to Plymouth."

Reeves started to go, then stopped and returned with a question. "Shall I mention the mincing of the Yanks, sir?"

"Of course! What the hell do you think I'm about?"

"I only meant...."

"Never mind what you meant. Do it!"

The Number One fled to the radio room and had the report sent.

***

"When do we get to Plymouth?" Liam asked. He could figure it out for himself but he needed something, anything, to open communication with Bradford.

"A half hour," Bradford answered. He was seated at his desk, his head lowered just enough to be noticeable to Liam.

"Would you like me to have the steward's mate bring you a cup of coffee, Commodore?"

"No, Liam, but I wouldn't mind a drink. A good stiff one."

"Neither would I. The Limeys have it. The Russkies have it. Prohibition's been repealed everywhere but in the U.S. Navy."

"Reach under my pillow, Liam," Bradford told him.

Liam knew immediately what Bradford was indicating, but it surprised him that he would flaunt naval regulations.

He walked to Bradford's bunk and groped under the pillow until he felt the bottle. Pulling out a fifth of Old Crow, he went to the sink and poured the Bourbon into water glasses.

"Nobody's perfect," Bradford remarked with a sly grin.

"Here you go, Commodore." Liam handed his superior the drink.

Bradford took a heroic gulp, sat back and waited for the whiskey to work its warmth.

Liam imitated Bradford, taking a bigger swallow than usual. He wretched slightly and coughed, then like the commodore, sat back and waited. "I thought you'd be angry with me," Liam commented finally.

"What for?"

"Siding with Cadgett. I'd feel better if you read me off."

"I won't do that."

"You've treated me like a son and at the first test of loyalty I went against you."

"You spoke your mind. I can't criticize that."

"And Cadgett? Do you consider him a good naval officer?"

Bradford did not reply.

"He's a near psychopath, sir," Liam said.

"Now, now, Liam," the commodore answered.

"In peacetime, men like Cadgett end up in psychiatric wards or prison cells," Fitzpatrick said. "It's only in wartime that society pretends their sins are virtues and finds a use for them."

"Lieutenant, Cadgett is a first rate officer, the kind who inspires a fighting spirit in his crew."

"I agree, sir," Fitzpatrick stated. "He's a fine officer so long as he must answer to men like you."

"You mean to men who have outlived their ability to command a ship in combat?" Bradford inquired.

"I'm sorry, sir. I didn't mean it that way."

"The question is, who makes the better decisions when men's lives are at stake -- the Cadgetts or the Bradfords?" Bradford continued. He rose wearily from his chair and almost lurched to his bunk, where he lay on his back, his head propped up by a pillow, and took another long gulp of Old Crow.

"Commodore..."

"Yes?"

"At that moment, sir...at that moment, all I could think about was saving those men in the water."

"Would you have disagreed with me if you knew that my orders were to proceed to port if attacked, without stopping to pick up survivors?"

"Yes, I would."

"You'll never make a naval officer, Liam. Never. Here, pour me another."

"You sure you want more?"

"Yes, I'm sure."

Liam took the bottle from the desktop and poured the commodore some bourbon. Bradford refused to accept the niggardly offering and waved his glass until Liam poured him more.

"So you believe Cadgett was right, I mean, morally right?" Bradford asked, and peered at Liam waiting for his reply.

"If I may, sir. I believe with a Catholic teacher I revere: 'Nobody is doing right who acts against his will.'"

"That doesn't sound quite right to me."

"I know. There's no hope for me as a naval officer."

Bradford forced a laugh.

"The war bring all types into the Navy," Bradford opined. "But the men who are running the show, thank goodness, are the right ones. The Halseys, the Nimitzes, the Spruances..."

"I'm sure you are right, sir."

They both went quiet.

Suddenly, Bradford broke the silence. "Nora mentions you in her letters."

"I'm glad. I hope she'll be my friend."

"From the tone of her letter I'd say she's interested in something more than friendship."

Liam remained silent.

"How do you feel about it?" Bradford asked.

The direct question was the last thing Liam expected from Bradford. He wasn't sure what the commodore was after.

"I must admit, sir, that I am attracted to Nora. More so than any woman I have ever met. But there's a wrinkle in the fabric."

"Someone else?"

"Yes, someone else."

They were quiet again. Bradford drank some more and Liam finished what was left in his glass.

"How many men do you think we lost today, sir?" Liam asked.

"I wouldn't be surprised if it were a thousand."

"Oh, my God!"

"For me, for Cadgett, for a lot of people, things will never be the same."

Chapter XV

Admiral Lundy was a man who understood much and revealed little. It was Lundy who was Bradford's superior and who had done the overall planning for Exercise Mongoose. It was only natural that he would join Admiral Romney in meeting the *1525* when it docked in Plymouth.

The moment the gangway touched the dock, Lundy and Romney hurried to meet Bradford and Cadgett who were waiting for them on the deck.

While Lundy stood aside, his eyes bruised with pain, Romney seized Bradford by the shoulders and with tears in his eyes kept repeating, "I'm sorry. I'm sorry."

"Bad luck," Bradford muttered.

"I wish luck were all that had gone bad," Lundy said.

"There's going to be a shower," Romney declared. "One huge shower of shit."

"You can bet on it," Lundy concurred.

Romney noticed Cadgett standing by, saying nothing, watching his superiors deal with the aftermath of a catastrophe.

"Captain," Romney said. "You must immediately warn your crew not to mention what happened in the Channel to anyone. Not a word."

Lundy, his face twisted with anguish, explained. "If word of this gets out, if it becomes known that our loaded ships are vulnerable to German attack so close to England, it will affect demoralize the invasion force."

Romney added, "The importance of secrecy cannot be over emphasized. The success of the invasion itself may depend on it."

"I'll take care of it, Admiral," Cadgett said and walked quickly up to the wheelhouse.

"Now hear this," he barked into the microphone. "This is the captain speaking. All hands muster aft on the tank deck. How!"

Five minutes later, Cadgett faced the one hundred and five officers and men of his crew. No one ordered them to fall in, so there was a mixture of officers and men crowded before Cadgett, who stood on the raised platform at the rear of the tank deck.

Cadgett addressed the men. They could tell how serious he was by how he spoke. His hillbilly accent broke through the more general speech he used to be better understood.

"I've had you all muster here because I don't want no one on the dock to hear me. What happened this morning is never to be spoken of. Not even among yourselves. You don't tell your buddy. You don't tell your momma. You don't tell nobody. A General Court Martial with the power to hang your ass waits for the man who talks. Keep your mouth shut tight as a fish's ass--and that's watertight."

He turned to leave. He found Bradford had followed him and was standing nearby. "Now, Commodore Bradford, the flotilla's flag officer, would like to speak to you," he said.

Bradford, surprised by the unexpected courtesy, exchanged places with Cadgett. He looked down at the crew and saw something in their eyes he had not seen before. They had been exposed to scenes that would never leave their minds, pictures that would flash back into their consciousness ten, fifteen, fifty years from that day. They would see the blackened bodies carried by the swells. They would see what the face of a drowned man looks like. Most of all, they would have experienced a fear so deep that it loosened bowels and opened bladders. And they had learned that the fear of showing fear was the most stressful emotion of them all.

"Well done," Bradford said, and walked off with the first hint of what soon would become a slight stoop.

CHAPTER XVI

Admiral Romney sat in his office chatting with his aide, Lieutenant Commander James Wright, until he could delay no longer. Wren Claudia Wakefield had been waiting in the anteroom for more than half an hour. It was time to pay the price of command.

"Send her in," he instructed his Wren secretary.

Romney found himself looking at a young woman of about twenty. She shone with a pleasant pinkness that was compelling, the kind that looked freshly scrubbed even after a couple of sets of tennis.

"Have a seat," Romney offered.

Claudia chose the chair nearest his desk and settled into it.

"Yes, sir?" she whispered.

Romney glanced sadly at his aide, then shuffled papers on his desk.

"Ahhhh," he said, "Ahhhh...there's been a...well, a dust up in the Channel. Warning messages were radioed to a Yank convoy that E-boats were in the vicinity. The Yanks did not hear the message...because they were tuned to the wrong frequency...."

Romney paused and looked at Wright with eyes that implored help.

"They were tuned to the wrong frequency because we gave them the wrong frequency," added Wright, coming to his assistance.

Claudia Wakefield went pale. Her small, almost

childlike fingers lying on her lap, jerked slightly, then trembled.

"Am I in trouble, sir?" she asked.

Romney said, "Let's just say it was one of those balls-ups that happen in wartime."

Wright glanced at Romney with an unmistakable look of sympathy.

"I won't deny I'm relieved, sir," Claudia sighed. "Very relieved."

Wright intervened again. "Where are you from, Wakefield?"

"Yorkshire, sir. Harrogate."

"You don't have a Yorkshire accent."

"Harrogate is one of those exceptions."

"Harrogate, eh? Never been there."

Romney interrupted. "Tell us how the wrong frequency happened to appear in Convoy M-6's orders."

All at once Claudia poured tears. "It must have been a typing error, sir."

"You mean you had the correct frequency on the message form, yet typed the incorrect one?"

"I did not have a completely legible number on the form, sir. It was somewhat blurred. I typed the frequency I thought the lieutenant told me."

"Which lieutenant?"

"It was my fault, sir."

"What was the man's name, Wakefield?"

"Dobson, sir."

"Well, thank you very much indeed," Romney said. "You know him, Jim?" he asked.

"Yes, sir."

"A reliable man?"

"Quite."

Romney picked up a pencil and scribbled a note. "Dobson articulated the number?"

"Yes, sir," Claudia answered.

Romney scribbled again. "Incorrectly?"

"Correctly."

"You heard him wrong?"

"I heard him correctly. I incorrectly remembered what he told me, sir."

194

Romney sat back and said nothing. Wright leaned forward.

"You heard him correctly yet you remembered it incorrectly. Is that what you're saying, Wakefield?"

"Yes, sir."

"You say the number was blurred. You received it in that condition from Dobson?" Romney asked.

"No, sir. It was blurred by spilled tea."

Wright smiled grimly and shook his head. "How ridiculously English. Tea causing the sinking of two ships and the crippling of a third."

"Never mind, Jim..." Romney commented by way of reprimand for what he considered frivolous and uncalled for.

"You spilled tea on the order?" Romney questioned.

"No, sir. Evans placed my tea cup on the message form. The cup jiggled and a little tea spilled from the saucer."

"She jiggled it?" Wright said.

"Yes, sir. I should have forbade her setting my tea there. I was remiss in not doing so, sir."

Romney stood up and pulled himself to his full height. "You may go, Wakefield, but stay on the base for now. Just until we've had time to sort things out."

"Thank you for being so understanding, sir. You don't know how guilty I feel about those poor Yanks."

"Yes, well, thank you for your help."

Claudia Wakefield stood up, saluted and left. Outside the admiral's office, she found Evans waiting her turn to be called in to face Romney.

"Prepare yourself, Priscilla. That tea you spilled blurred the numbers I typed and a lot of Yanks died."

Evans paled, then began to tremble. She started to say something to Claudia but Claudia did not wait. Instead she strode angrily away.

"Let's get Evans in here," Romney told Wright.

Wright walked to the door and motioned to the Wren secretary to send Evans in. Prompted by Romney's secretary, Evans got to her feet and virtually forced herself to enter Romney's office.

"All right, Evans, sit down," Romney said.

Shaking with fear, the young woman almost did not make it. About to faint, she took small measured steps to the chair and sank slowly into it. She began to sob, her body wracked with agony.

For the first time Romney lost his patience. "See here, Evans, stop this unmilitary behavior."

"It's my fault, sir, all those Yanks. It's horrible, horrible."

"Take it easy, woman," Wright soothed. "Mishaps in civilian life turn out to cost lives in wartime. Doesn't help going to pieces."

She removed a handkerchief from her pocket, dabbed at her eyes and wiped her cheeks. "I'm sorry, sir," she answered, making an effort to pull herself up in her chair.

"That's better," Romney said. "Now, Evans, tell us how a cup of tea ended up on the message form."

"I placed it there, sir."

"Why there, Evans?" Wright asked.

"Because we always place the tea next to the typists so they can reach it easily, sir."

"So *everyone* does it that way?" Wright wondered.

"Yes, sir."

"Ah, there, you see, Commander, *everyone* does it that way," Romney said to Wright.

"Thank you for acknowledging that, sir," Evans said.

"And you jiggled it. The cup, I mean."

Evans hesitated. "I know it sounds crazy, sir, but I cannot recall my hand shaking. The cup just... jiggled...it jiggled. I don't know why."

Romney glanced at Wright from the corner of his eye. Wright glanced back at him and shrugged.

Romney said, "You can leave now, Evans, but do stay on the base until all the facts have been gathered. We may have to speak to you again. Just to clarify something or other."

"Am I going to be punished, sir?"

Wright smiled and shook his head. "Not to worry," he promised.

"Thank you, sir." Evans replied, sounding doubtful.

She rose unsteadily from her chair and fairly stumbled to the door.

In the anteroom, she once again began to cry. Romney's secretary helped her out of the room, then returned to tell a waiting Lieutenant Commander Neal that he could go into the admiral's office. He was expected.

***

"All right, Neal, what happened?" Romney demanded. There was no preliminary politeness. Romney then peremptorily waved him to a chair.

Neal, a short, brown-eyed Ulsterman in a worn uniform, appeared to assimilate the mood and girded himself for the worst.

"The *Espadon* was holed by a Yank landing craft that slipped its moorings and went adrift," Neal said. "Because of the damage, I ordered her to stay behind for repairs, sir."

"And how bad, may I ask, were the damages?" Romney questioned.

"Not grave, but in high seas she could have shipped water, sir."

"You saw the damage with your own eyes?"

"No, sir."

"Then how did you determine it was bad enough to ship water?"

"The position of the hole, sir."

"You knew she was only one of two escorts for eight LSTs?" Wright asked.

"I did. Yes, sir. The way you say it makes it sound as if I made a hasty, unconsidered decision. I did not, sir. I specifically asked what kind of mission she was assigned. Her captain told me it was not a combat mission, sir, just an exercise."

Romney rose from his seat and walked around to the front of his desk. He leaned against it and spoke directly to Neal at as close a distance as he considered seemly.

"You knew there was German torpedo boat activity in the Lyme Bay area before?" He paused, then continued. "Of course you knew. We all knew."

"I knew, sir."

"Well, go on."

"That was weeks ago. With the huge amount of activity around our southern ports and the increase in the number of destroyers patrolling the Channel, we assumed that Jerries would be crazy to send E-boats out."

The reply so angered Romney that he took a step closer to the man, then bent over until their faces were only inches apart.

"Crazy? They were crazy to start this war. They were crazy to invade Russia. They were absolutely out of their minds to declare war on the United States."

"Sir, just a week earlier Exercise Gray Wolf was held in that exact area and there wasn't a peep out of the Nazis," Neal replied.

"You fancy yourself quite the strategist, don't you, Neal?"

"I stand by my decision, sir. It was a well-considered decision, sir. If things went wrong, well, they went wrong, sir."

"Yes, we know, Neal, things go wrong," Wright interjected.

"Indeed, things go wrong," Romney agreed.

"Those are my exact feelings, sir," Neal stated.

"You passed the loss of the escort on to Plymouth, did you not?" Romney asked.

"I did, sir."

"How about to the Americans? Did you report

the loss to Admiral Lundy's staff?"

"Why, no, sir."

"Why not? They're the ones who were most concerned."

Neal's eyes darted around the room. He licked his lips. His face flushed red and he began to perspire. He stirred in his chair, but he did not answer.

Romney looked at Wright who smiled a dreary, resigned smile.

Romney returned behind this desk and sat down wearily. He ran his hand over his pained face, looked down at his desk, then up toward Neal.

Romney said, "Neal, stay on the base until we get this thing sorted out. We may want to ask you some more questions later, so we'd like you to be available. We'll call you when we need you."

Neal's eyes narrowed.

"Am I under house arrest, sir?"

"Of course not."

"Am I restricted to quarters, sir?'

"See here, Neal, relax. Play some snooker. Drink some beer."

Neal sprang angrily to his feet. He saluted with extra precision, did an about turn and marched out of the office.

"Obnoxious, isn't he?" Romney said.

"He's a gem," Wright replied.

They sat in silence for some moments.

Romney drummed his fingers on his desk, reached for a Players and lit it. "Like one?" he asked Wright.

"No, thank you, sir."

"You know, Jim," Romney continued, ground out his cigarette after only one puff, then reached for his pipe, "They tell me Eisenhower is hopping mad. Some of the missing officers had been bigoted. They knew their part in the invasion plans. What if Jerry fished one out of the water alive?"

"I don't suppose they can change the day and place of the landings at this late date."

"Of course not. Impossible. There are millions of men and hundreds of ships getting ready to move as we speak."

"Of course. My question was rhetorical. But what now?"

"If you were a Yank, what would you think, Jim? They've suffered as much as a thousand dead, near as we can tell. They're going to want to see some action on our part."

Wright folded his arms and let his head drop a couple of inches. "When we were running the show we would have demanded action."

"Jim, it would be foolish of us to let our pride get in the way of facing things squarely."

Wright stiffened. "Yes, sir."

"The Russians have already won the war. We're spent. Bankrupt. Fighting on borrowed money. Yank money. We haven't the money or the will to hold onto our colonies after the war. We'll be a second class power. Living on past glory. We're going to need American protection from the Russians from now on."

Wright looked away from Romney.

Romney pressed down on the tobacco in the bowl of his pipe with his thumb. He looked up at Wright's slightly turned head. "Don't you think it would be unwise to appear to be callous about the loss of American lives?"

"A well-crafted explanation might do it."

"I don't think so," Romney answered. "I'm going to recommend to the Admiralty that we accept full responsibility for what happened. Let's get their people off the hook. They'll be grateful. I know I would be."

"All right, then, sir, what are your orders?"

"Place Neal under arrest. Arrange for a court martial. I want the Americans to see our blood flow."

"And the women?"

"Leave them alone. Going after them would only make things worse."

200

***

There was a feeling of expectancy in the room. The surviving captains of the flotilla that had come to grief and their flag officer, Charles Bradford, had been invited to meet with Admiral Romney at the Plymouth Navy Yard.

They thought they would be getting a briefing on their invasion assignments. Instead, they were treated to something more akin to a cocktail party.

An attractive Royal Navy Wren took orders for their drink preferences and bade them make themselves comfortable in chairs that had been brought in for the occasion.

While the drinks were being mixed, Romney rose from behind his desk.

"I bid you welcome in the name of His Majesty. Our esteem for our American allies could not be higher. Before me I have the skippers of the landing craft that will land the main force on one of the beaches of France--the name of which for now must remain secret."

Disappointment was felt by the American skippers, but it was tempered by the prospect of being served drinks at an official naval function, something that was unthinkable in the United States Navy.

"We called this meeting to extend the apologies of the Royal Navy for the disaster in the Channel that cost the American Army and Navy some eight hundred men and officers."

The American skippers, some still haggard and emotionally bruised from their ordeal, fidgeted in their seats.

"We all know that these things happen in war. Still, we sincerely apologize. We all know human beings are vulnerable to mistakes and errors of judgment. Still, we accept culpability. Now let us put this behind us and unite to finish the great task before us. Let's all have a drink and some good old sailor fun. A Royal Navy rating will now distribute your drinks. She's quite pretty, and knowing the reputation of you Yanks, she has been ordered not to get too close."

A few of the skippers forced themselves to laugh politely.

Bradford, beamed with good will and stood up. "Thank you, Admiral, for your unnecessary apology and your good wishes. We, too, have made mistakes. We, too, have lost ships through human error. We accept your invitation, don't we fellows? Bring on the booze!"

Romney surveyed the seated Americans. He could recognize that his words had a salutary effect. The attitudes of the assembled officers had softened somewhat, and it appeared they were prepared to give the British the benefit of the doubt.

The one exception was Captain Cadgett. He had remained sullen throughout the speech and this provoked Romney's discomfort. Romney gazed with curiosity at the grim man seated before him. Cadgett, from what Bradford had told him, was certainly not the type who could be commissioned in the Royal Navy. Still, Romney understood the problems the Americans had had. Having to build the largest army, navy, and air force in their history in a matter of months made it necessary to choose presumed competence over other considerations. Romney had come across captains of American vessels whose parents were not even born in the United States--men with Polish, Italian, German and Jewish names. That the Americans were willing to entrust naval vessels to them was an astonishment to him.

Romney kept staring at Cadgett until all the drinks were distributed. Cadgett did not take the drink, instead, the Wren placed it in his hand, and he had to grasp it or let it fall to the floor.

Bradford rose, drink in hand. "Gentlemen, a toast to the brave men of Exercise Mongoose who died.

God rest their souls."

The captains all drank as one. Some were teary eyed.

"Gentlemen, to the United States Navy!" Romney said.

The captains took their second gulp.

"Gentlemen," Bradford said, holding his drink high, "to the Royal Navy."

Again the captains drank, except for Cadgett, whose voice suddenly drawled through the room. "They're shining us on, guys."

Cadgett placed his drink on the floor, stood up, maneuvered his way through the captains, and strode from the room.

Chapter XVII

Graying Admiral Harvey Q. Hickman had a favorite restaurant and a favorite waiter. Nothing short of a Japanese invasion of California could stop him from lunching at the Cafe Corneille with his friend and confidant, Rear Admiral Jon Riffel.

They had no sooner settled into their reserved booth when the waiter had their double-olive martinis before them.

"I heard Chief Henderson amusingly refer to these as thigh openers," said Hickman holding up his glass.

"He's a colorful old coot," Riffel said.

"Went asiatic years ago," Hickman chuckled.

Hickman downed his martini in several quick gulps. "First one of the day always goes fast."

"Are you ready to order, Admiral?" the waiter asked.

"Are we?" Hickman asked Riffel.

"Maybe one more," Riffel replied.

Hickman placed his now empty glass on the table, "One more, Albert."

"Yes, sir," the waiter acknowledged, and slipped away.

"Anything new on M-6?" Riffel asked after sipping his drink.

"Meant to tell you," Hickman answered, his eyes searching the room for acquaintances. "Romney says the British are accepting responsibility over what they call the 'balls up' at Strangull Strand."

"That's a relief. I was afraid they'd try to wriggle out of it. I don't trust the bastards."

"Set them right down, Albert," Hickman told the waiter, who had just arrived with their second round.

"Yes, sir," the waiter replied.

"Romney's got integrity. There's no denying it," Hickman remarked.

"Integrity, hell. It's a political decision."

Hickman picked up his martini and sipped at it. "Could have been drier."

"Want to send it back?" Riffel asked.

"No," Hickman answered, "I'll suffer with this one."

Riffel popped one of the two olives skewered on his toothpick into his mouth and returned the other to his glass.

"Do you wish to start with the salads, gentlemen?" Albert asked.

"I don't feel like it today," Hickman said.

"Neither do I," Riffel concurred.

"We'll skip them, Albert."

"As you wish, sir."

"Will you be having soup? It's your favorite today, Admiral. Vichyssoise."

"Yes, okay, Albert."

As soon as the waiter had gone, Hickman told Riffel what he had been thinking about for the past few days. "Riff, do we really want the British to take the blame? It will stir up a lot of resentment against England around the country."

"It's us or them, isn't it?"

"Your soup, gentlemen," Albert said and pushed their martinis aside to make room for the vichyssoise.

The two ignored their soup, while sipping their drinks in silence for a while. They thought about the consequences of the Exercise Mongoose disaster. It wasn't the first catastrophe they'd had to deal with.

There was Pearl Harbor, of course, but there was also the destruction of the Asiatic Fleet at the beginning of the war and the devastating defeat at Savo Island.

"You know what's going to happen the moment the war ends?" Hickman asked. "The public will be screaming for the Army to be sent home. Then what's to stop the Russians from overrunning the entire European continent?"

"Not a damn thing."

"We're going to need Britain as a base. Do you think it would be wise to turn American public opinion against them with the Mongoose story?"

"I see your point."

"I don't feel like soup. Do you?"

"Not really." He signaled the waiter.

"Albert, take the soup away. Bring us a couple of New York cuts with baked potato. That all right, Riffel?"

"Sure."

Hickman finished his martini and dabbed his lips with a napkin.

"By the way, any further reports on the number of casualties?"

"From Mongoose?"

"Yes."

"It's going to take a while. The Army has a lot of checking to do. There were people aboard from various units. We're more sure of Navy casualties, though. Together you've got figure seven to nine hundred. Somewhere in there."

"This entire Strangull Strand thing has been a pain in the neck."

Riffel ran his hand over his bald spot. "Lower than that," he said. "How are we going to handle this? Disobeying orders should qualify--what's his name?--Cadgett for a court martial. But Bradford's refusal to go back and save those men doesn't sit well with me."

"Not with me either," Hickman agreed.

Riffel went on, "But we can't tolerate disobedience."

"True enough."

"Admiral?" Riffel inquired, looking at Hickman.

"Yes?" Hickman responded.

"D-day is almost on us. Suppose we lay in the weeds. Hell, Cadgett or Bradford, or even both of them might be dead a couple of weeks from now. If that should happen, why, we'll just blink the whole thing out.

"No," Hickman said. "Let's get them back here. Let's amputate before gangrene sets in. Lundy, too. After all, technically Mongoose was his responsibility."

***

Admiral Lundy delivered the news in person. He came aboard LST *1525* on the twentieth of May and asked to see Bradford and Cadgett separately.

When Lundy told Cadgett he was being recalled to Washington, the *1525*'s skipper was momentarily disoriented. His head reared up and his eyes darted around the cabin. It was as if he had been told news that could not possibly be true, yet had to be dealt with.

"What's all this about, Admiral?" he asked after he had recovered sufficiently to speak. "I inspected this ship when she was still on the rails. I took a few dozen high school boys and turned them into an efficient crew. I sailed two thousand miles to take part in this invasion, and now, at the last moment, I'm being relieved of my command?"

"You're not being relieved," Lundy replied conciliatorily, "your're being recalled."

"Recalled for what?"

"For consultations."

"Couldn't it wait until after the invasion?" It's only days off."

"I'm afraid not, Cadgett. Washington evidentially deems it more important for you and Bradford to return right now."

"Bradford, too?" Cadgett muttered. "It's about Strangull Sands, isn't it? They want to grill me about Bradford's cowardice."

"I don't think this is the time or place to discuss the matter," Lundy declared with just enough edge in his voice to signal that their meeting was over.

After the Admiral left, Cadgett, in a fit of anguish, slammed his fist into the bulkhead.

"I'm not going to be part of the invasion," he moaned. "I'm not going to be part of it."

Having stonewalled Cadgett, Lundy made his way to Bradford's cabin.

"Hello, Charlie," he said after Bradford admitted him.

"Well, Admiral Lundy. Glad to see you. Must be important. New orders?"

"Yes, as a matter of fact." He slid into the vacant chair facing Bradford. He paused, and with almost imperceptibly trembling fingers, removed a bent cigarette from a nearly empty pack of Camels. He deliberately took his time lighting it. He smoked silently while deciding the best approach to take.

"Charlie," he said to the now thoroughly expectant commodore, "you're not going to like this, but you're needed back in Washington."

"When?"

"Now. The first ship back." He aimed his glance directly into Bradford's eyes. Through a cloud of exhaled Camel smoke he explained, "It's Strangull Strand, Charlie. The Navy wants to know exactly what happened and they want to know it straight from your lips."

"Look, Admiral," Bradford stated, "Cadgett did what he thought was right. Yes, he disobeyed my orders, but it was under the extreme stress of the moment. I hate to see this happen to him."

"Charlie, I don't know what's going to happen to him. All I know is that they want you home.

"Cadgett, too?"

"Cadgett, too."

"The invasion would have looked good in his record. I'm sorry for him."

"I'm sorry, too," Lundy agreed and left, feeling as if a whirlwind had spiraled through him, taking with it his innards and his breath.

Later that night, with his own recall orders on the desk before him, Admiral Lundy shot himself.

Chapter XVIII

"Wakefield here."

"Claudia," Cadgett said.

"Verne, is it you?"

"It's me all right."

"Thank God you're alive. I've heard things, terrible things. When I didn't hear from you I thought...."

"I'm safe. Not a scratch on me."

"How did you manage to get this call through?"

"An American intelligence officer here did me a favor."

"Kiss him for me," she said.

"He's ugly as a mud fence."

"Oh, Verne. It's so wonderful to speak to you. When will I be able to see you?"

"I just got orders to report back to the States."

"They're sending you to the Pacific, aren't they?"

"A worse place than that—Washington."

"You sound so depressed," Claudia observed.

"Well, I am. They want to rob me of being a part of the most important military action in history. I'm sick about it. I've been throwing up all morning."

"I'm sorry, Verne. But you can't stop me from being happy about it. I don't want you dead."

"There are worse things," he replied.

"Verne, what's going to happen?"

"This is what's going to happen: The minute the war's over I'm coming back to marry you."

"Oh, Verne. That's a lifetime away."

"I don't care how long it takes"

"None of this sounds real, Verne."

"Never mind the palaver. You're going to wait for me. And I'll be back."

"Verne, I may be the one responsible for. . ."

"No more discussion," he said emphatically. "That's the way it's going to be. I'll write to you as often as I can. You do the same. I love you, Claudia." He then hung up.

Chapter XIX

Bradford and Liam boarded the Washington train at Pennsylvania Station unaware that Cadgett had boarded the same train.

Bradford and Liam took a double seat facing an ample, unsmiling, middle-aged woman who had deposited her luggage on the unoccupied seat next to her.

The train left the station on time, roaring through the tunnel into New Jersey, then lurched noisily south.

Cadgett and several other passengers who had boarded the train just before it left the station were disconcerted to find every seat filled. The late-comers split into two groups, one scouting for empty seats forward, the other to the rear. Several passed the seat-hogging woman, frowning angrily at her selfishness. They could not muster the energy to remonstrate with her and charged ahead. Not so Captain Cadgett.

"Hello, fellahs," Cadgett interrupted when he saw Liam and Bradford.

Obviously surprised, they fell into silence.

"Mind putting your bag up in the rack and letting me sit down?" he asked the woman.

She glowered at him.

"Here, let me help you with that," he said and before she had a chance to reply he swung her bag into the rack above.

"I'm sure, you all will excuse me," he said, squeezed past their knees and dropped into the seat.

They remained silent for the first minutes of the journey as the train passed industrial areas partially obscured by oil refinery smoke.

After a while, Cadgett realized Liam and Bradford were not going to take the initiative.

"It's four long hours to D.C.," he said.

Bradford did not answer, but Liam, out of habit of replying when addressed by a superior officer, mumbled something Cadgett interpreted as an affirmative.

"We're both going to be on the carpet for Strangull Strand. Who do you think they're going to come down on, Commodore?"

"We'll just have to wait and see, won't we?" Bradford said.

Cadgett leaned back, musing. He pursed his lips and crossed his legs. "If Strangull Strand leaks to the newspapers, the Gold Star Mothers are going to be howling for your blood."

"Excuse me, Captain," Liam intervened, "can't we just leave it alone until it happens. This isn't doing you or the commodore any good."

"It's all right, Liam," Bradford answered. "I know the Navy. I'll earn their respect, not their enmity."

Cadgett smiled and shook his head. "You think so? Politics are more important than policy in Washington. They're going to fry your ass."

Bradford smiled back at Cadgett. "We shall see whose ass will fry, as you so charmingly put it."

Nothing more was said the rest of the way to Washington. Once there, the men sorted themselves into one cab behind the other, and played tag with each other right up to the entrance to the Pentagon. The same elevator lifted them up to the same floor and anteroom where they handed their orders to the same WAVE petty officer outside Admiral Hickman's office. They sat down across from one another, waiting to be summoned.

"The Admiral will see you now," the WAVE spoke up, nodding in Cadgett's direction.

He smiled Bradford's way, then proceeded to march into Admiral Hickman's presence.

Hickman rose to his feet when Cadgett entered. He walked around the desk and pumped his hand.

"I've been looking forward to meeting you," he said. "I want to thank you personally for saving those sailors."

Flattered, Cadgett inclined his head slightly toward Hickman. "Thank you, sir."

Hickman stepped back as if to take the measure of the man.

"We're lucky to have men like you, Cadgett. You proved the Alamo spirit is still alive in the American people."

Embarrassed, Cadgett wished the admiral would skip the compliments and get down to business.

"Hello, Cadgett," intruded Riffel's voice from the corner of the room. It was a skeptical, mocking in its tone, condescending in its cadence. "I said, 'hello', Cadgett."

Cadgett found himself looking at a pale man of about forty years old. His face was deeply creased by vales of skin. His eyes were the color of ice, so light was their blue coloring. His aspect was grim, the kind of officer, some thought, who could order destroyers to charge battleships without giving the certainty of their destruction a second thought.

"I'm Admiral Riffel," the man announced, then swung one lanky leg over the other, leaving a long, slim shoe waving back and forth in the stale office atmosphere. "Sit down," Riffel ordered Cadgett. "Take that chair over there. You'll find it more comfortable. Would you like a cigar?"

"Thank you. I don't smoke them," Cadgett answered.

"They're Cubans. The best. The boys down at Gitmo get them for me real cheap." He slipped his hand inside his coat jacket and pulled out a leather cigar case. He carefully removed one and rolled it between his thumb and index finger, enjoying its crackle. After biting off the end, he placed it delicately between thin, purple lips, picked up a lighter from Admiral Hickman's desk, and set the cigar aglow. A haze of smoke drifted to the ceiling where it flattened, then dispersed into nothingness.

"Cadgett," Hickman said, "there's a good chance that six months from now the war in the Pacific will be over. We have a few stunners in the wings. Surprises for the little yellow bastards."

"If we're going to invade Japan that soon, I hope you'll waste no time letting me get my ship out there, sir."

"We may not have to invade, Cadgett. We may just not have to."

"It's hard to believe they'd give up, sir," Cadgett commented, shifting his gaze from Hickman to Riffel, who was peering at him intently.

"They just might," Hickman smiled knowingly. "They just might. And when they do, we'll have to build a new Navy to meet the realities of new and unimagined technologies."

Cadgett stirred in his chair, his eyes receptive for more. "It will be exciting to be part of it, Admiral," he said.

In response, Hickman turned his eyes to Riffel.

"Yes," Riffel agreed, puffed on his cigar, and added, "We'll be needing scientists and technicians in the new Navy. Men with degrees in physics, electronics, all sorts of disciplines, all sorts of technologies."

He paused, removed the cigar from his mouth and held it about twelve inches from his nose as if inspecting it for flaws. He knocked off the ash into a tray on Hickman's desk.

"Unfortunately, Cadgett, there won't be much room for men like you. Or, I regret to say, like me."

"I beg your pardon, sir?" Cadgett said.

Hickman leaned forward and looked Cadgett in

the eyes. "Admiral Riffel's right, Cadgett," he said. "There'll be no need for a lot of men like us."

Cadgett rose in his chair, then thought the better of it. He felt his forehead go damp. The implications of what the admirals were saying churned his stomach, and for the first time that he could remember he was stunned by someone's words alone.

"If you're asking me to resign, you're wasting your breath," he said belligerently.

Riffel leaned back in his chair. His words were like that of a lawyer so certain of his case that he need not raise his voice or change his posture.

"Tell us, Cadgett, why did you disobey Bradford's order? Were you convinced that you were a braver officer than Bradford, a man who in the First World War sank a U-boat by ordering his four-pipe destroyer to ram it? Did you think you're smarter than Romney, who helped plan the destruction of the French fleet at Oran? Are you more intelligent than Admiral Lundy, who did much of the planning for three successful invasions? Tell us, Cadgett, is that why you disobeyed orders under combat conditions?"

"No, damn it," he replied.

"Then who are you to have put the success of the Normandy invasion at risk? Did you, in your great strategic wisdom, understand the possible consequences of what you were doing? How many ships you endangered? How many lives you gambled with? Well, do you, Cadgett, do you?"

"I had to save those men," he retorted without flinching. "I couldn't leave them to drown."

"You wanted to save those men, did you?" Riffel sneered, his voice rising for the first time. He uncrossed his legs and rose menacingly from chair. "I'll tell you what you wanted to save, Cadgett," Riffel said. "You wanted to save your commission. You were afraid you'd be reduced back to enlisted ranks after the war ended. So you had to do something spectacular, something to make you so big a hero that the Navy wouldn't dare take away your rank. The

Navy made you a gentleman, Cadgett. Men obeyed you. Women laid down for you. Civilians respected you. Colored boys waited on you. You couldn't stand the idea of going back to being a peckerwood."

Cadgett's accent reverted to that of his youth. He was no longer a naval officer but a defiant backwoodsman. "With all due respect to your rank, sir, that's batshit. Pure, one hundred percent, unadulterated batshit. And I'll see you in hell before you get my resignation!"

"Maybe you'll see me in hell, Cadgett, of you refuse to resign I'll see you first serving ten years in Portsmouth for disobeying a superior's orders in a combat situation."

"Obeying orders will be even more important in the future, Cadgett," Hickman explained. "Every man will have to obey unquestionably, even if it results in the killing of millions and certain retaliation that will destroy their own families. What's more, disobedience is a virulent disease that spreads. Do you read the Bible, Cadgett? 'By one man's disobedience many were made sinners. Romans 5:19:.' We can't have it, Cadgett."

Cadgett stared straight ahead. He was like a battered boxer, staggered, struggling to remain on his feet.

"Before you go, Cadgett, I have something for you," Hickman said. He lifted a stack of papers from his desk revealing a small dark box. He pushed it slowly, almost reverentially across the table as near to Cadgett as he could.

With a look of surprise Cadgett reached down, but stopped just before he touched the box.

"Go ahead," the admiral said, "pick it up."

Cadgett took the box, and after drawing it to himself looked up questioningly at Hickman.

"Open it," the admiral instructed.

Cadgett opened the box to find himself staring at a Navy Cross. He could not take his eyes from it.

But he did hear Admiral Hickman's words. "Bradford put you in for it."

"Bradford?" Cadgett exclaimed incredulously.

"Yes, Bradford. He's one of your greatest admirers."

Cadgett snapped the box shut and the sound echoed like a gunshot in their now silent presence.

Hickman rose and walked around his desk to stand facing Cadgett. He put out his hand. It was impossible for Cadgett to mistake the sincerity of the act. Cadgett shook it.

"Good luck, Cadgett. You're a brave man."

Cadgett could not reply. He left the admiral's office clutching the box in his hand.

Erect as an Annapolis midshipman on parade, Cadgett marched in silence past Liam and Bradford in the anteroom and out the office door.

"What do you think happened?" Liam asked Bradford.

"I couldn't tell from the look on Cadgett's face."

"Admiral Hickman will see you now, Commodore," the WAVE receptionist interrupted.

"Good luck, Commodore," Liam said, and shook Bradford's hand.

"Thank you, Liam," he replied and walked into the Admiral's office.

Admiral Hickman had asked for one of Riffel's cigars and had it lighted by the time Bradford was seated in the chair before his desk.

"Good to see you again, Bradford," Hickman told him.

"Nice to see you, sir."

"Hello, Bradford," Riffel called from his corner of the office.

Bradford turned his head in the direction of the voice and recognized Riffel, a man he had never liked.

"Oh, yes, hello, Admiral." He forced a smile.

For a few moments Hickman seemed to struggle with himself about what to say to Bradford. He put his cigar in the ashtray then picked it up again, took a puff and returned it to the ashtray. "Bradford," Hickman said, "you acted with reason. You are to be congratulated for your self-discipline. It must have been excruciating for you to go against your instincts and order the ship back to England."

"It was not an easy decision, I admit. But I know I did the right thing."

"True. True." Hickman moved his chair back farther from his desk. "What are your plans, Bradford?" Hickman asked.

"Plans? BUPERS makes my plans."

Hickman lifted his chin and stared down his glasses at Bradford.

"Surely you intend to resign?" he asked.

"Resign?"

"Why, yes."

Bradford went cold. He heard Riffel stir in his chair and turned his head in his direction.

"Of course you realize," Riffel intervened, "no officer or enlisted man would feel comfortable serving under you again?"

"What?"

"They'll believe you would abandon them in a crisis," he pointed out. "That's nonsense of course, but that's what they'll believe."

Bradford paled at the thought. He considered what Riffel was saying and could not accept it.

"Is that the general opinion?" he asked.

"It is," Riffel replied.

"Is it?" Bradford asked Hickman.

Hickman nodded.

Riffel said, "Think of public relations, Bradford. If you remain in the Navy, every family who lost a kid in the war will want your scalp. And I don't even want to think about what Congress can do with this. When the war ends they're going to want to dismantle the Navy. We're going to have to fight for every penny. We can't afford ill will."

Bradford felt a tremor go through his body. His

shoulders sagged as he considered the admirals' logic.

"You've turned everything upside down," he protested bitterly.

Hickman answered, "Technically, no one disagrees with you. Emotionally everyone does."

"You're a liability Bradford." Riffel continued, "We can't give you a sea-going command. We can't give you a command ashore. That would be interpreted as an insult to you. It would impair the respect of the men under your command."

Bradford could not think of a reply.

"We're promoting you to rear admiral," Hickman said. "It will be dated well before your resignation. Good luck, Bradford. May I shake your hand?"

Bradford, as if in a trance, leaned over the desk and shook the hand of the now standing Admiral Hickman. Then, ignoring the proffered hand of Riffel, he walked to the door with all the dignity he could muster.

Before leaving, Bradford turned. "I could have ordered the *1525* to return and become a hero to fools. But what if D-day had failed because the tanks we landed were not there to repel a German counter attack?. Wars have been lost for less. What would the families of the dead have said about me then? And what would history have said about me for disobeying an order and that prolonging the war a year, even two? I could have drowned a continent with the blood that would have been shed because of my disobedience. My conscience is clear, Admiral." He tossed them a casual salute and left.

Outside, in the anteroom, Liam hurried to his side. "How did it go, Commodore?"

"I'll tell you on the way to the Wiltshire Hotel. Nora should be waiting for us there. She shouldn't have taken off from school to come down here. But I'm touched by her concern."

"There's the elevator," Bradford said, and hurried to catch it. They were the only passengers.

Bradford frowned and shook his head from side

220

to side.

"Bad news?" Liam asked.

"I'm afraid so."

A pained look came to Fitzpatrick's face. "Oh, no," he said, almost in a whisper.

"I have to resign," Bradford said.

"They cashiered you?"

"No. Even got a promotion."

"It's insane," Liam responded as they crossed the lobby to the exit.

"There's logic to it."

"Logic? What logic?"

"Navy logic."

They came out of the building into a dark day. Clouds the color of gunmetal stirred above as if in a cauldron.

Suddenly Bradford and Fitzpatrick halted, astonished by what stood before them. It was Cadgett, at stiff attention, saluting. The commodore, recovering from his surprise, brought his heels together and whipped his right hand to the visor of his cap. Bradford and Cadgett stood immobile, eyes locked, while Fitzpatrick gaped at the unimagined tableau. Cadgett and Bradford stood there for several long moments, Cadgett holding his salute, Bradford maintaining his return gesture. Finally, Cadgett dropped his arm. After Bradford did the same, Cadgett walked to him and extended his hand. Bradford, without hesitation, took it. They stood and looked at each other for a long moment.

"Thank you for returning my salute, sir," Cadgett said.

"Thank you for offering it."

"May I ask how you fared?"

"*Out* for obeying orders. And you, sir?"

"Out for *disobeying* orders."

"Permit me to buy you both a drink," Cadgett offered. "I think we all deserve one after that ordeal."

"We must get to the Wiltshire Hotel," Bradford told him. "Why not join us?"

"Thank you, sir. I'll do that."

Cabs began to line up for the change of shift. Liam hailed one.

They crossed the bridge and drove in heavy traffic to the hotel where they found Nora Bradford waiting, a half finished martini on the table before her.

Bradford embraced his daughter.

"Welcome home, sailor" she said, and kissed him on the cheek.

"Piece of cake," he replied.

"You owe the shore party fund ten dollars for that," Cadgett said.

Liam smiled at Cadgett's rare attempt at humor, then he and Nora embraced like old friends.

"Glad you're home safe, Liam," she said softly.

"So am I," he replied.

Bradford introduced Cadgett.

"Verne Cadgett, my daughter, Nora."

"Glad to meet you, ma'am."

"So you're the notorious Captain Cadgett?" She said as she inspected him thoroughly.

"That I am."

"Why, you look almost human."

He laughed.

They joined Nora at the table. Bradford suddenly grasped his daughter's wrists.

"There's no other way to do this but straight," he said.

"What? What is it?"

"I'm resigning."

"Oh, my!" she burst out, "That should change things for the better. You'll be coming home for good now."

"No, Nora, it won't change anything. Your Mother and I have agreed to a divorce. And I'm leaving for England as soon as I can get permission and transportation."

"I don't understand," Liam said.

"I met a wonderful lady while we were in England. I asked her to marry me and she agreed to as soon as I get out of the Navy. I'll be living in England. She won't leave Britain."

"Where did you meet her?" Liam asked.

"Romney's headquarters. You may have seen her when you were there. The blonde Wren who had a desk to the right of the Admiral's office. Her name is Claudia Wakefield."

Cadgett recoiled as if struck by a great weight. "Claudia Wakefield?" he mumbled.

"Yes. Remember her, Captain?"

Cadgett did not reply for a while.

"Yes, I think I do remember her," he finally said.

A searing anger surged from Cadgett's gut and ate its way into his chest. Fed by his jealousy and feelings of betrayal, it grew in his breast like a protean beast. Blood drained from his face until it shone white as a death mask. He squinted at Bradford. The Commodore was smooth, pink and glowing. His eyes were blue-white, like drops of spilled milk. He was *them*. Cadgett would have to kill him. It was only right, only fair. It was justice. Bradford had taken his most precious possessions, his woman and his pride. He would smash his glass into Bradford's face then grind the shards into his eyes with his heel as Bradford lay prostrate on the floor. Cadgett's muscles tensed. He wrapped his right hand around his glass. He closed his left hand into a fist. He tightened until he felt his nails press into his flesh. Ignoring the pain, he dug his nails even deeper into the ball of his thumb. Blood seeped to the surface and pooled in his palm. He welcomed the pain and wished it would last forever. He moaned, but inaudibly. The blood trickled down his fingers and struck the floor in small magenta drops.

"Congratulations," Cadgett choked out.

"Will I be seeing you, Liam?" Nora asked.

"No, I'll probably be transferred to some other ship, then it's out to the Pacific, I'm sure."

"And after the war?"

"Mullen and I -- one of the officers on the *1525* --

Mullen and I are planning to open a restaurant in San Francisco. I have the money. He has the idea. I hope you understand."

"How nice for you both." Nora at long last grasped the source of her failure to gain Liam's love. She berated herself for not having recognized the truth earlier. Well, so be it. To hell with him! She tried not to show her hurt or even her concern. She steeled herself, forced a smile, and turned her attention to Cadgett.

"And how about you, Captain?"

"Maybe I'll go into the whiskey business."

"Selling?" Liam asked.

"No, makin'," he replied.

They called the waiter and ordered drinks, which they sipped in silence. They fidgeted with their glasses, then dried their hands with paper napkins. After a while, the men paid the check then all walked glumly into the grayness of the threatened day. A light snow began to sweep toward them, and wind-driven litter swirled around their ankles. A flock of scavenging pigeons scattered into flight. The snow turned to sleet and umbrellas opened among the passers-by like suddenly blooming black flowers.

The melancholy group lingered on the pavement outside the hotel bar, wishing each other good luck.

"I'll be going back with Nora to wind up my affairs in Massachusetts," Bradford said.

Nora turned her attention to Cadgett and surreptitiously scanned his face. She marveled at the tenseness of his jaw and the impenetrable metal of his eyes. He extended his hand to bid her goodbye and she looked down to grasp it.

"Captain Cadgett," she said in a near whisper.

"Yes?"

"Do you like horses?"

224